TREACHERY

RISING

SHERRYL D. HANCOCK

Published by Vulpine Press in the United Kingdom in 2018

ISBN 978-1-83919-259-3

Cover by Claire Wood

www.vulpine-press.com

To the lovers and fighters of the world. Keep doing what you do, it's worth it in the end!

Also in the *MidKnight Blue* series:

CHAPTER 1

In Sacramento, California, Joe had managed to find a townhouse he could rent for the two months he'd been there. The house was actually downtown; he hadn't been able to find anything closer to the college.

The second day he was in town, he met with the Chief of the Bureau of Narcotic Enforcement and the Chief of the Sacramento Police Department. He found that he liked both men. John Davies, BNE's chief, was very down to earth, and the Sac PD chief, Arthur Martinez, had come up through the ranks so he understood the day-to-day struggle his officers faced. Joe had impressed both men with not only his knowledge of gangs but also with his expertise in weapons. He was able to provide the pros and cons for both departments' issued weapons as well as suggest some additional benefit to other weapons.

By the end of the session, John Davies had invited Joe to attend an upcoming Special Agents in Charge meeting for the Bureau of Narcotic Enforcement coming up in San Diego. "The invitation extends to Lieutenant Chevalier as well," he had added.

The next morning was Joe's first appearance at the Sacramento Police Department's academy. It was their first day at the range, and although the sun was out, the breeze was chilly and the air a bit more crisp than Joe was used to.

"I thought you came from England. It's cold there, isn't it?" Jessica asked, grinning at Joe as he pulled on his FORS jacket.

"I haven't lived in England for goin' on fourteen years," Joe retorted, giving her a sour look.

"Bad mood today, Sergeant?" Jessica said.

"No, I just hate mornings, especially when they start at 6:00 a.m!" He'd had to get up at 6:00 to have time to get showered and dressed and be able to make the hour's drive to the academy.

Joe retrieved his gear bag and looped his newly polished duty belt around his arm. He'd had to hunt for the duty belt he had used when he was in the sheriff's academy, having not been on the streets for very long as a deputy; the belt had gotten put away and forgotten about. He had found it the week before and had some work done on it to make it presentable again. The academy class was dressed in jeans and their academy sweatshirts, each with their names on the back. The students were milling about, waiting for the course to start. When Joe walked onto the range, someone yelled, "Fall in!" The candidates organized themselves into two rows and stood at attention.

"Oh shit," Joe said, getting a flash from the past, when he'd been in the academy, which received a number of chuckles. "Look," he said, addressing the candidates, "I'm probably gonna get my ass chewed for this, but I'm so long out of an academy, all this formality scares me. So why don't you all relax and we'll be just fine." A murmur went through the group, and there were more than a few small applauses. Finally, everyone seemed to relax.

"First of all, the name's Joe Sinclair. I'm a sergeant with the San Diego Police Department. I've been a cop for over ten years. I graduated from the San Diego sheriff's academy at the top of my glass in marksmanship. Trust me, boys and girls, it's come in real handy in my line of work. Are there any questions?"

One young man raised his hand. "Sir?"

Joe looked at him and shook his head. "If that was your question, then the answer's no. Don't call me sir—call me Joe, or Sinclair. I'll answer to either."

The young man laughed with rest of the group and shook his head. "No, sir—I mean, Joe—I was curious what your average range score was, so we know what to aim for."

"Three hundred," Joe said simply.

"But that's a perfect score." Disbelief colored the young man's voice.

"And?" Joe replied. The student just shook his head. "Anything else?"

"Have you ever been shot?" a young woman asked.

"Yes, I have," Joe said. "And trust me, it hurts."

He looked around, seeing that no one else seemed ready to ask any questions. "Now, what I do want to do, before we do any shooting, is to take a look at everyone's duty weapons. I don't go for salutes and I don't play drill sergeant, but I will run anyone's ass outta here if your weapon is not properly cared for. So why don't you prepare your weapons for inspection. For those of you who don't know what that means, I want your magazine removed, your slide locked back, and your barrels pointed at God. And believe me, if I find any chambered rounds, God's gonna be the only one that can help ya." His voice was serious, and the group shuffled nervously as they complied with his request.

Joe checked the weapons, and after making a few comments to some of the candidates in terms of better cleaning, he told them all to get comfortable. He spent the next two hours talking to them about their weapons, what they could and could not do and what would cause them to malfunction. He told them about what he planned to teach them and what he expected of them. "I'm not looking for perfect marksmanship. I just want you to be proficient with your weapon." He looked around the group seriously. "Your weapon should be your last line of defense, but if you get down to using it, you better know what you're doing, because I can guarantee you one thing—if you're afraid to shoot, your adversary won't be, and that'll get you killed."

At that, he told everyone to take a break.

While on break, Joe called to check in with Midnight. Luckily, she was in her office for a change.

"Hey there," Joe said when she answered the phone, sounding harried.

"Joe, hi, how's it going in cow town?"

"Fine, except for the fact that I'm cold and damned tired!"

"Cold I get, but why tired?"

"Because I had to get up at six o'clock in the fucking morning, that's why!"

"Sorry, honey, that's the breaks. Oh, by the way," she said, changing subjects as fast as ever. "Speaking of fucking and up, you did."

"I what?" he asked. "How'd I manage that all the way up here?"

"Well, you did it before you left. I just didn't know it till you were gone."

"What happened?" he asked, concerned now. He didn't like to make mistakes; they were usually dangerous.

"Well, remember that raid you planned?"

"Yeah," he said slowly.

"Well, you forgot to figure in their hit on that cop supply shop a month ago."

Joe closed his eyes, his face showing his irritation at himself. "They had armor," he said, following her lead. "Shit, I didn't remember that. So what happened—did everything go all right?"

"Well, duh, Joe, you don't think I'd be so calm if I'd lost someone, do you?" Midnight's voice showed the strain she was under. Having him gone was harder than she had expected.

"No, that was a dumb question, I know," he said. Another thought occurred to him. "Rick must've been all-time pissed."

"Well, that's a fair assessment, since he got a pretty good crack on the head from someone he thought he'd disabled with a chest shot." Her voice was tinged with anger, and Joe understood that she must have been terrified when she realized what had happened.

"Night," he said, knowing there wasn't much he could do at this point. "I'm sorry. Shit! My mind wasn't on the job, and I know that can't happen. I'll pull it together while I'm up here, I promise."

"Yeah, I know you will," Midnight said, regretting her anger. She knew what he was going through; she herself knew better. "Look, don't sweat it. Nobody got hurt bad, and we shut 'em down."

"Yeah," Joe muttered, still irritated with himself.

The class noticed their instructor was distracted when he began the second part of the morning. The rest of the day was spent doing drills. Joe's mind wouldn't let him rest, wouldn't let him forget that he'd screwed up, and it could have cost him his best friend's life.

He told Jessica about it a couple of days later, while they were at lunch. She told him about the shootout that had scared her off the street.

"I don't know what I'm gonna do next week when the shooting at the range is real. I get real jumpy around it," she was saying.

Joe was watching her. "I'll get you through it, and I'll get you back on the street before I leave Sacramento."

"In two months?" Jessica shook her head. "I doubt that."

But Joe nodded. "You wait, you'll see."

****

The following week at the range, not only did Joe stand behind Jessica when the shooting started, but he put a reassuring hand on her shoulder. At the end of the day, after the candidates had gone, he stood with her, having her draw her weapon and fire "dry" rounds. He'd had her remove the ammunition clip, the "magazine," and remove the chambered bullet by pulling back the slide and locking it into place. As night approached, he actually had her shoot the nine rounds her gun contained. After the first couple of rounds she didn't jump every time the gun fired. By the last shot she had actually hit the target in a respectable area.

"See?" Joe said, grinning at her.

"Oh my God," she said, laughing. Out of impulse, she turned and threw her arms around his neck, hugging him. Joe hugged her in return and smiled down at her.

"Told you, didn't I." His eyes held a twinkle in them, and Jessica had to agree with him.

"Yeah, yeah, I know," she said, waving away his confidence.

"We'd better get goin'."

They followed each other in their respective cars. Joe remained behind her, yet another gallant thing that Jessica found endearing about him. Twenty minutes into the drive, on a lonely strip in the middle of nowhere, a car coming the opposite way took the oncoming curve too wide and came within inches of colliding with Jessica's car. Jessica veered off just in time, but lost control of the car and rolled down the embankment at the side of the road. The other car overcorrected and ended up skidding away and colliding with a streetlight.

Joe slammed on the breaks, avoiding the accident. He jumped out of the car, running headlong down the embankment. Jessica's car had ended upright, but the engine was on fire. Joe tried but couldn't get her door open. Jessica looked dazed, but she was conscious, and Joe yelled for her to cover her head. Taking a step back, Joe kicked in the driver's door window. Knocking the remaining glass out with his arm, getting cut in the process, he managed to pull her from the vehicle. He carried her up the embankment and put her in the passenger side of his car. Another car had come along by then, and its driver was trying to help the driver of the other car involved in the accident. Joe knelt in front of Jessica, touching her face. "Think you can radio this in?" he asked. She nodded. Joe stood and ran over to the other vehicle.

"The doors are all jammed!" the man trying to help yelled. Then he pointed to the small child in the back seat. There were two adults in the vehicle as well.

"Shit!" Joe said, seeing that both adults were unconscious and the child was crying. "We gotta get these doors open, now."

"Yeah," the other guy said, "but how?"

Joe kicked out the rear window, on the one side where there wasn't a passenger. Bracing one booted foot beside the door handle, he grabbed ahold of the interior handle and, with every ounce of strength he had, he yanked as hard as he could. The metal groaned and gave a little, but did not open. Joe was panting by this time, as adrenaline surged through him. He could see that smoke was starting to fill up the interior of the car, and he knew he had to get this door open. Taking a deep breath, he pulled with all of his might. The door gave with a metallic shriek and Joe fell backward to the ground. He hit his shoulder on a large rock, but he didn't even feel it. He jumped up and climbed into the car to get the young child.

"It's okay," he told the little girl, "I'm gonna get you out of here." With as much gentleness as he could, he lifted the girl out of her seat. He handed her to the man waiting just outside and went back in after the other two people. The smoke in the car was thick by this time, and he began to cough as he moved to the passenger. The other man had handed the child off to yet another passerby who had stopped to help. Joe could hear sirens in the distance, but he didn't think they'd get there before the car was engulfed in the flames that had started flicking out from under the hood. He checked the woman on the passenger's side and found that other than a nasty cut to the head, she seemed okay to move. Grabbing her under the arms, he pulled her over the seat and moved to hand her out. He went to the driver and noted that the steering wheel had been jammed downward in the accident; there was no way to get the man out without damaging his legs or worse. Joe climbed over the seat, and then, leaning back toward the passenger door and making sure the man's body was out of the way, he kicked at the driver's door, trying to shove it open. Two kicks later the door came open and the other man was able to pull the driver out.

Joe was coughing, with tears from the noxious fumes running down his face, which was smudged from the smoke. He slid out of the car and helped the other man to carry the driver. Ten seconds later, they were thrown to the ground as an explosion ripped through the gas tank. Joe lay in the wet grass, staring at the fire. He was breathing heavily and still coughing from the smoke he'd inhaled. When he stood to move the driver again, his vision swam and he began to feel lightheaded. With all the effort he could muster, he made it to the top of the embankment before he sank to his knees, his vision going dark. The last thing he heard before he passed out was Jessica yelling his name.

Joe woke a little while later. He had an oxygen mask over his face, and he was staring up into Jessica's eyes. He lay on the grass, his head on her lap. After a few moments, Jessica noticed he'd come to, and she called the paramedic over. Joe was already reaching up to rip the mask off as a wave of nausea hit him. He rolled off Jessica's lap and, staggering to his feet, walked a few feet away before being sick. He walked back to Jessica and sat down heavily in front of her. The dizziness came over him again, and he moved to lie back on the grass, but Jessica tugged him over so his head rested on her lap again. She stroked his hair. "You okay?" she asked softly.

"Yeah," Joe said, his voice hoarse. "If the world would just stop spinning."

"Close your eyes," Jessica said. Joe did, and he felt better.

A little while later, a car drove up and two men got out. One of them was older, in his mid-fifties, and the other was about thirty-five. They hurried over to where Jessica sat with Joe's head on her lap.

"Jess?" the older man said, concern written all over his face.

Jessica looked up. "Daddy!" she said, surprised to see him, although she realized she shouldn't be—he monitored the police radio even at home. The other man was her brother, Henry. Joe moved to get up so that she could stand and show her father she was okay. Upon standing, however, Joe found it necessary to sit again immediately or risk passing out.

"You okay, son?" Gerald Harland asked Joe.

"Oh yeah," Joe said, waving the other man's concern away. "I just did my first day as a fire-eater, and I'm not quite up to the task."

Gerald Harland laughed, as did his son and daughter. "You should have seen it, Dad!" Jessica said. "Joe rescued me and he got that family out of their car right before it blew up!"

Joe was shaking his head.

"Yes, you did!" Jessica said, wanting to give Joe all the credit she thought he deserved.

"Whatever," Joe said, resting his arms on his knees and his head on his arms.

The next day at the academy, Joe was being hailed as a hero. The Sac PD chief even called Midnight to tell her what her officer had done. Midnight had texted Joe immediately.

Joe called her from his cell phone, since he was out on the range.

"So I hear you're a celebrity now!" Midnight yelled, trying to make herself heard over the sound of weapons fire in the background on Joe's side.

"Don't you start too," Joe said, gesturing to Jessica to watch the candidates as he walked far enough away to be able to have a civil conversation with his boss without yelling.

"Whaddya mean, don't start? From what the chief told me, you saved four lives."

"I don't think I'd go that far," Joe said.

"Well, the chief did."

"Well, obviously he's given to exaggeration."

"Yeah, right," Midnight said. "Are you okay?"

"I got a little singed, and I can't stop coughing, but other than that…" He trailed off as he laughed.

"You take care of yourself, do you hear me?" Midnight said.

"Yeah, yeah. So what's been going on there?"

"Well, for starters I've been asked to speak to Randy's academy class."

"And?" Joe said, sounding distant.

"Don't be a jerk, Joe. I know you want to know what's going on."

"Okay," he said, taking the bait, "what's goin' on?"

"Well, I haven't seen her, but I've heard that Randy's hanging out with that Sarah Dickerson and her brother. You know, Sergeant Dickerson from vice?"

"Yeah," Joe said, his voice cold as his thoughts churned.

"Well, I'm sure it's just because she's around Sarah a lot," Midnight put in, realizing too late that she shouldn't have brought up that Randy was hanging out with another man.

"Yeah, I'm sure too," Joe said, not sounding convinced.

They ended the phone call shortly after that. Midnight didn't want to risk saying something else she shouldn't.

As Midnight hung up, she muttered, "Shit."

"Shit what?" Rick asked, standing in the doorway to her office.

Midnight looked up at him and shook her head. "Nothing. What's up?"

"Just wanted to check in, see if you had any more on that bust, results and whatnot."

Midnight shook her head. "I did let Joe know about what happened. I also let him know you owe him one." She pointed to his head, indicating the fair-sized gash he had obtained from the raid.

"Trust me, I'll collect somewhere down the road," Rick assured her.

"Yeah, I'll bet…" Midnight said, trailing off as she saw Randy walk off the elevators with Sarah Dickerson trailing behind her.

Rick followed her line of sight. "What's she doing here?" he asked, mildly interested. He had come to find out what had been going on between Joe and Randy, by way of the rumor mill. Joe and he weren't back on friendly terms as of yet.

"Don't know," Midnight said. "But I guess I'm about to find out," she added, as Randy headed for her office.

Randy walked up to Rick, smiling at him. Rick nodded politely, then walked away. Randy didn't seem affected by his curt acknowledgement. She looked different, Midnight realized, as Randy stood at the door to her office. Midnight didn't smile, her face unreadable as she nodded to the chairs in front of her desk.

"Yes?" Midnight asked finally.

"I wanted to talk to you," Randy said.

"And you needed backup?" Midnight's eyes flicked to Sarah, disliking her on sight.

"No, Sarah's just here because we were out at the academy and we got done early," Randy explained, irritated that Midnight would think she needed someone to back her up when they talked.

Midnight nodded, not saying anything. She leaned back in her chair, looking from Sarah to Randy. "So talk," she prompted.

"I heard that Joe was involved in an accident up in Sacramento," Randy said, trying to keep her concern for him out of her voice.

Midnight nodded.

"Is he okay?" Randy asked, hating that she had to ask. But Midnight didn't seem forthcoming with any details, and the only thing she had heard was that a San Diego PD sergeant on assignment in Sacramento had been involved in an accident.

"He's fine," Midnight replied simply.

"Fine?" Randy countered, growing impatient. "That's all you're going to tell me?"

Midnight looked at Randy for a long moment, her eyes cool. "Well, I'm sure that if your husband felt that you gave a damn and knew where to contact you between parties, he would have called you." Midnight had heard more than she had let on to Joe, and the knowledge fueled her anger now.

"What fucking business is it of yours what Randy does?" Sarah put in accusingly.

Midnight looked at Sarah as if she had just noticed her. "And who the fuck are you?" she asked, her voice low.

"I'm Randy's friend, which is more than I can say for any of you people." Sarah's gesture took in the office outside.

"And how would you know?" Midnight asked, her voice still calm, but her eyes burning.

"I know more than you think," Sarah said, her face beaming confidence.

Midnight looked at the woman for a long moment, and then in a very controlled and businesslike voice, she said, "Obviously not, recruit. I happen to be a commanding officer in this department, and the current direction of your attitude is not only considered gross insubordination, but it'll also get you thrown out of the academy on your ass, if I want to do it." Midnight's voice was low, but the threat she made was very real. Sarah stared back at her as if not realizing who she had been talking to. Obviously she had forgotten her current position versus Midnight's rank. She closed her mouth, not willing to challenge Midnight's authority any further.

Midnight looked at Randy. The girl seemed a lot less confident now that her friend had been taken down a few pegs. In truth, she wished she had listened to Sarah when she had told her not to go to Midnight for the information about Joe.

"Now," Midnight said, her voice changing again, as if to punctuate who really had the upper hand here, her gaze steady on Randy's face. "If you want to know about your husband, I believe you have his cell number, and he currently has it on. Feel free to utilize it." With that, Midnight stood, a signal for Randy and Sarah to go.

Randy and Sarah did leave then. Once out in the car, Randy exploded. "How fucking dare she!" she yelled. "Tell me to text him, like I'm still his secretary."

"She is an A-number-one bitch, isn't she?" Sarah said, feeling very defensive after the verbal beating she had taken from Midnight.

Randy looked at her friend. "Yeah, except she was right. We shouldn't have gone to her office."

"Well, you know it's a gray area there," Sarah said, trying to rally her friend. "I mean, your husband works there, and you don't anymore."

"But Midnight is a lieutenant," Randy replied, realizing slowly that she was definitely on her own now. Midnight had sided with Joe—not that she would have expected anything else, but Randy knew she was alone now. The thought scared her a little bit.

She was living at Sarah's apartment now, helping with the rent. She still had her credit cards that Joe had given her, but she hesitated using them, except when Sarah talked her into it to buy some things for the apartment and to run a tab at the bar that they frequented very often now. Randy reflected on the change in her life, and in a way she liked the freedom from Joe's ever-watchful eye, which she had convinced herself had been stifling. But there were times when she missed knowing that if something bad happened, she could always turn to Joe. She had reasoned herself out of that worry by asking herself, "What could happen?"

Randy had seen Darrell since getting into the academy. He wasn't aware of her and Joe's split, and she was shocked when he told her he thought she was an idiot.

"Because of the money, right?" Randy had said. "Well, I'll get some of it when the split is formal."

Darrell had taken a long, hard look at her. "Are you saying you're going to divorce him?"

Randy stared back at her brother, never really thinking about it that way. The truth was, the idea of divorce was too final for her. She'd just gone along thinking that she'd go her own way, and when she knew what she wanted, she would do something more permanent. "I don't know," she said after a few minutes, shrugging. "Anything's possible." She sounded far more confident than she felt.

"Well, if you divorce him, you're even dumber than I thought," Darrell said, surprising Randy.

"What do you mean?" she asked, her eyes wide. "You want me to stay with him?"

Darrell nodded.

"You were the one that hated him—you tried to talk me out of marrying him!"

"That's when I thought he wasn't good for you."

"Oh, and now he is?" Randy said, angry and hurt that her brother wasn't supporting her. "You think he's so great? Well, if you knew what's been going on, you wouldn't think so anymore."

"What's been going on?" Darrell asked mildly.

"He's screwing around!" Randy said, sounding desperate to convince Darrell and herself that Joe was no good.

Darrell looked at her for a long minute, then said, "I don't believe it."

"What!" Randy all but screamed at him. "You don't believe it, or you don't believe me?" Her voice teetered on the edge of hysteria. Who else did she have if her own brother didn't support her?

"Believe who, about what?" Donovan asked as he came into the kitchen where Darrell and Randy were talking. He walked over and hugged his older sister. Donovan was a very tall twenty years old, and he still idolized Joe, so Randy assumed she'd get no support there.

Darrell looked over at Donovan. "Randy thinks Joe's cheating on her."

Donovan looked from Darrell to Randy. "No way!"

Randy sighed, having guessed Donovan's reaction. "Donovan Curtis, you wouldn't believe that Joseph Michael Sinclair the Fourth wasn't a fucking god if I told you it!" she said harshly. Donovan looked taken aback.

"Whoa, sis," he said, holding up his hands. "What the hell are they teaching you at that academy? Must involve a lot of assertiveness training, huh?"

Randy shook her head, sitting down at the kitchen table.

Darrell knelt down next to her. "Randy, we don't believe Joe would cheat on you because the guy loves you more than life."

"Yeah," Randy said quietly, "sure he does." She sounded unconvinced.

Randy spent the next two weeks talking to Sarah and Dick about it. They both managed to convince her that her brothers didn't know, that they had no idea how close Midnight and Joe were, that they didn't see how Joe reacted every time Midnight had the slightest problem. Dick was talking to her one night when Sarah was out. They were sitting on the couch in the apartment.

"I know it's hard to think about, Randy," Dick said softly, his hand touching hers, "but wouldn't you rather be on your guard against him breaking your heart?" He squeezed her hand. "I don't want to see that happen to you."

Randy looked up at Dick. She had become very close to him and his sister, out of necessity. Dick's brown eyes were warm and friendly, and she was so grateful to him for trying to keep her from letting Joe walk all over her. Every time she tried to make excuses for something else that Joe had done in recent months, Dick was there to support her side of it. When she talked about Joe's vehemence about her not being a cop, Dick was there to tell her she deserved to be able to do whatever she wanted in life, and that if Joe really loved her he had to love all of her, regardless of what he thought she had done wrong. Hadn't Joe made his mistakes? Randy had confided in both Dick and Sarah, telling them things she had never shared with anyone else. She had even admitted to them that she and Joe had made love the day she'd gone over to get her clothes. Dick had seemed angry. He told her that Joe was just taking advantage of her and that he wanted to confront the guy and beat his face in for her. Randy had told him that she didn't want him to do that, and Dick had gotten the distinct impression that she wasn't trying to protect Joe from harm.

Now, as they sat on the couch, Randy felt very comfortable. Of course, she had a few shots of Southern Comfort in her that Dick had offered her. She leaned back and was surprised to feel Dick's arm behind her neck. She looked up at him, and he smiled, almost shyly, as if she had caught him at something. Randy laughed, thinking of the drive-in scene from Grease.

"You're not going to give me your class ring, are you?" she asked, a little bit tipsy but happy to be laughing again.

"I don't think I have it on me," Dick replied, patting his pockets.

Randy snapped her fingers. "Darn!" she said, smiling up at him.

Dick looked down at her, lying against his arm, and he moved his face down to hers almost timidly. The tentative touch of his lips on hers surprised her, and Randy felt his hand tighten on his shoulder. She kissed him back, her head feeling a little light from the alcohol. Within a few minutes, he had laid her back, her head resting on the arm of the couch, his body covering hers, as their kisses turned more passionate.

Randy made herself concentrate on kissing Dick, even though her mind was screaming at her that she was cheating on Joe now. He did it first, she thought angrily as she reached up to pull Dick's body even closer to hers.

They made love that evening, and afterwards he kissed the back of her neck tenderly as he fell asleep, holding her from behind. They lay on their sides on the couch, with her in front of him. Randy fell asleep eventually, with tears on her cheeks.

****

Midnight got wind just over a week later that Dick Dickerson and Randy were "together" now, and she knew when she took one look at Dickerson the day she showed up at the academy to talk to the class that he and Randy were sleeping together. Dickerson gave her a smug look, knowing that she and Joe were partners, then turned and winked at Randy. Dick Dickerson, as one of the members of the vice squad, had also been asked to talk to the academy. It had just so happened that he was there the same day as Midnight.

Midnight felt the anger boiling in her blood—she almost couldn't see straight. She glanced at Randy and was surprised when the younger woman returned her look with an openly hostile one.

Midnight told the class about FORS and what they did. She explained the methods they utilized were more often than not ad lib, not by any books. At the end of the discussion, Midnight asked if there were any questions.

One young man raised his hand, looking very taken with the lieutenant. "Yes?" Midnight asked, pointing to him.

"Are there any specific areas we should concentrate our efforts in if we want to make it onto your team?" It was obvious to everyone that the young man wanted to get on her team for a reason, as they all laughed. Randy, Midnight noticed, looked disgusted. She looked right at her as she answered the question.

"Yes," she said, "you want to perfect your hand-to-hand combat skills—they come in very handy in a gang fight. And sometimes that's the only way to take these people down."

"I'll bet those skills get a bit rusty after a lot of disuse," Sarah put in, a challenge in her eyes.

Randy seconded the comment. "Especially after sitting at a desk for a long time, some skills must get harder to use." Her eyes danced with the anger and distaste she apparently had for Midnight now.

Midnight seemed to consider the comment, then looked straight at Randy. "You wanna try me?" she said, her voice cool. The challenge was received by the class as they clapped; they had no idea what was really going on. They thought it would just be a practical exercise.

The group moved to the gymnasium. Randy was looking pretty sure of herself, and Sarah had been talking to her since they left the classroom. Midnight stood alone on the mats, wearing her usual attire of jean, boots, and cotton shirt. She had changed nothing, just removed her weapon from the small of her back and handed it to one of the instructors.

"Anytime," Midnight said.

Randy strode to the mat and faced Midnight. Midnight looked at the class standing watching them. "In FORS, most of your one-on-one confrontations with gang members will take place between you and the leader. The attack will come from head on." She looked at Randy. "Charge me, and try any kind of punch you think you can handle." Her voice was low, but she still spoke instructively.

Randy hesitated, then ran at Midnight, surprising the leader of FORS with an uppercut that caught Midnight on the left side of her jaw. But to Randy's surprise, Midnight didn't even flinch. Instead, she grabbed Randy's still-extended arm, stepping in toward Randy while moving to put her back to her. Midnight followed through by flipping her to the ground. Randy stared up at her, surprised at Midnight's strength, having never had a physical confrontation with her before.

Midnight's eyes were narrowed as she looked down at her partner's wife. For show, Midnight extended her hand to Randy to help her up, as the rest of the class clapped. After a long moment, Randy decided she would look even worse if she didn't accept Midnight's assistance—after all, it was only supposed to be an exercise. When Randy was on her feet, with Midnight standing very close to her, she could almost feel the heat of Midnight's anger on the side of her face as Midnight's voice grated in her ears.

"You may be screwing my partner over," Midnight said, her voice a harsh whisper, "but don't ever fuck with me again, little girl." Her emphasis was on the last two words, and Randy walked away feeling a cold knot of fear in her stomach.

Midnight turned to Sarah. "You wanna try me too?" Her voice was light, but the look in her eyes told Sarah she had every intention of completing this here or somewhere else. Sarah nodded, her ego making her brave. She outweighed Midnight by a good thirty pounds, and she was much stronger than Randy. Sarah stepped forward, her eyes on the leader of FORS.

"You may have gotten the better of Randy," Sarah all but crowed, all puffed up with her own confidence, "but you'd better watch yourself with me, Lieutenant." The class cheered again. Sarah had been their leader in hand-to-hand combat. Randy watched from the sidelines, not sure what she wanted to see. Part of her wanted to see Midnight taken down a few pegs, especially after what she had said to Randy, but another part of her wanted to be able to hold on to the image of Midnight being invincible.

Midnight did not counter Sarah's words, not given to bragging before she beat an opponent. "Now, sometimes we have gang members catch us off guard, on things like a raid. So Sarah, I want you to come at me from behind."

Sarah smiled even wider, knowing that with her extra weight plus the fact that she was at least four inches taller than Midnight, she would easily beat her, especially from behind. Midnight waited for Sarah to get into position. Without warning, the bigger woman brought her arms around Midnight, clamping down on her arms with surprising strength and lifting Midnight off her feet. Instead of struggling against the hold, as Sarah had expected her to do, Midnight waited until Sarah began lowering her to the ground. With a grunt of effort, Midnight brought a booted foot down and back, cracking Sarah in the shin and causing her to let go of Midnight to reach for her own leg. Midnight whirled around like lightning, bringing her knee up to just under Sarah's chin. With extreme control born of experience, Midnight halted her knee's progress, knowing that continuing the move would seriously injure the other woman.

Midnight wanted to prove a point, not break the woman's jaw. Sarah straightened immediately, taking a step back from Midnight as if she now considered her a threat. The class broke into a roar of cheering and applause. Midnight watched Sarah closely, half expecting the woman to try something else, just to get even. Sarah limped back to the group, saying nothing. Midnight's eyes followed her, and when she looked back at Midnight to find her watching her, she saw the barely veiled threat in her eyes. Midnight did not take kindly to people messing with the people she loved, and as far as she was concerned, Joe loved Randy, and by definition, Sarah was screwing with that.

CHAPTER 2

After the accident, Joe had been invited to the Harland home for dinner. The first night he met the Harlands he found himself being scrutinized by the middle brother, who was about ten years Joe's junior. Gary Harland was suspicious of Sergeant Sinclair; he was very protective of his baby sister, and he didn't want anyone to hurt her. At one point Gary caught Joe alone in the sitting room of their elegant older home. Gary, who was a full head shorter than Joe, walked over to the Englishman.

"So," he said, being a straightforward kind of guy, "you're not after my sister, are ya?"

Joe looked at the younger man, surprised by his frankness. He held up his left hand, showing him his wedding band. "Not allowed to be," he said simply.

"Yeah," Gary said, his face showing that he wasn't convinced, "but you and I both know that doesn't always mean shit to a cop."

"It does to this one," Joe replied, turning and walking into other room.

Gary watched him go with a new respect for Joe Sinclair.

During dinner the discussion ranged from the progress at the academy to Jessica's progress at the range. Martha remarked later about the pride in Joe's face when he told them how well Jessica was doing. Then they talked about San Diego, and whether Joe liked living there. They asked if he owned a house in San Diego, to which Jessica had made a choking sound.

"Shut up," Joe had said, smiling at her. The rest of the family looked on, waiting for an explanation.

"You see," Jessica said, gesturing with her fork, "Sergeant Sinclair is what we would call filthy, stinking rich."

There was silence in the room as the Harlands waited to be told that it was a joke. But that was not forthcoming.

"Really?" Gary asked. Then the youngest brother, James, stepped in.

"Just how rich is that, Sergeant Sinclair?" James' eyes were wide in mock wonderment.

Joe looked at them both and grinned. "Very," he said, raising his eyebrows suggestively. The other two men broke into raucous laughter.

"Boys!" Martha Harland said, giving Joe a stern look as well, at which he feigned obedience.

"Sorry, ma'am," Joe said, his eyes down, a grin still on his face, much like the ones on Jessica's, Gary's, and James' faces.

"Like hell," Martha said, surprising Joe.

They ate in companionable silence for a while. Then Martha looked over at Joe, noticing his wedding ring for the first time.

"You're married, I see," she said pleasantly.

Joe nodded slowly, not looking exactly happy.

"Why the long face?" Martha asked, a mother to the very core.

"Long story," Joe replied, waving away her concern. Martha got the hint and dropped the subject.

That evening, Joe sat in the bedroom of the townhouse and thought about calling Randy. The thought irritated him. He hadn't been able to stop thinking about the fact that she was hanging around with Dick Dickerson. Joe didn't know much about the man, but he had heard that the vice cops tended toward womanizing, since they were used to dealing with hookers and the like. Joe's imagination had wandered just about everywhere, but he knew if anything happened, Midnight would tell him. It galled him that he was now in this position, not sure whether or not he should call his own wife. Part of him was afraid of what she'd say in any case.

The next morning he was tired and not in a good mood. He and Jessica were riding together since the accident, at first because her car wasn't fixed and then because he felt better driving her home rather than letting something like that happen again. Jessica had told her father about Joe's insistence that while he was around, he didn't want her taking chances like that. What Joe had come to calling the Harland Gang approved highly of Joe's opinion, and were happy that he was driving her to and from Yuba College. The family thought a lot of Joseph Sinclair, and felt that either way he was good for Jessica, especially if he could restore her nerve to get back on the street.

"Problems?" Jessica asked, eyeing him as he drove.

"Not new ones," he replied.

Jessica was silent for a while. Then she looked over at him again, noticing that he was twisting his wedding band around with his thumb, deep in thought. "Is it about your wife?"

Joe looked at her for a long second. "Have I said anything about my wife?"

"No," Jessica said. "That's what made me think you were having problems in the first place."

Joe shook his head. "I really gotta get you into the detective's test," he said, his voice reflecting his amazement.

"What's her name, anyway?" Jessica asked, happy that he thought so much of her deductions and that he seemed halfway willing to talk to her about his problems.

"Randy."

"Interesting name," Jessica said, with no malice in her voice. "How did you meet her?"

"She was my secretary."

"Oh, so it was like that, huh?" Jessica said, a knowing look on her face.

"Like what?" Joe asked, looking over at her.

"Sexual harassment," Jessica said, with the beginnings of a grin.

"It was not!"

"Well, not really, because obviously she liked it." Jessica was laughing by this time, and Joe just shook his head at her.

"So what happened?" she asked.

"She wanted to become a cop, and I didn't want her to," Joe said, shrugging.

"So you left her because you didn't want her to be a cop?" Jessica asked, incredulous.

"No, she left me, but I'm not really sure why."

"So why didn't you want her to be a cop?"

"Because I'm worried about her, that's why."

"What's there to worry about?"

"If she got hurt, or worse." Joe hesitated, obviously thinking about what could be worse. Then he said, "I don't know what I'd do."

"So what makes you think she'll get hurt? I mean, don't they train you people very well down there?" There was a note of humor in her voice, and Joe couldn't help but smile.

"Probably just as well as they train 'em up here," he said, an oblique reference to her shooting incident only two months into her street time.

Jessica grinned. "Point taken," she said, noting Joe's satisfied smile. "Why are you so paranoid though?"

Joe was silent again for a few moments, then he said, quietly, "Because I know what it's like."

"Like?"

"To lose someone you love," Joe said. Jessica could see the pain written on his face.

"Who, Joe? Who did you lose?"

"I lost my parents to a rival gang member. He wanted to get me." Joe shook his head. "He got them instead."

"How old were you then?" Jessica asked, surprised to be hearing this.

"Almost twenty-one."

Jessica was silent for a while. "So that's when you became well-off," she said. "And then you moved here?"

"In a roundabout way, yeah."

"And you became a police officer," she continued, and Joe nodded. "And how long have you and Lieutenant Chevalier been partners?"

"A little over seven years."

"No wonder," Jessica said.

"No wonder what?"

"Well, she seems to know you pretty well."

"She does, we're pretty close."

"How close?" Jessica asked, detecting a different tone in his voice.

"Well," Joe began, looking just slightly embarrassed, "we've been as close as you can get."

"That explains a lot."

"What's that supposed to mean?" Joe asked, curious rather than defensive.

Jessica shrugged. "Just that you seem very defensive of her, and that's usually territory covered by a lover, not a friend."

"Well, we aren't lovers anymore. Haven't been for a long time now. We just have a different kind of relationship." He looked over at Jessica. "You gotta understand that Midnight and I come from some seriously damaged backgrounds, and we've basically needed each other to survive all this time."

"And that's okay with your wife?" Jessica asked skeptically.

"Randy knows about me and Midnight. If Midnight needs me, I'm there. It's the same for her," Joe replied, defensively this time.

"Knowing about something and being okay with it are two different things, Joe."

Joe looked at her. "She's never said anything," he said, sounding less sure of himself suddenly.

Jessica shrugged. "When did the trouble between you two start?"

"When she told me she wanted to be a cop."

"When was the last time Midnight needed you?" Jessica asked evenly. She knew she was getting into unchartered territory now, and that she had to be careful.

"Midnight's married, for God's sake!" Joe said, not willing to play the game.

"You said that was for the time being."

"It is, but—"

"But, did you have to be there for your partner lately? And where did that leave your wife?"

Joe was quiet for a while, thinking back. He thought about the night Randy left. He'd asked about Midnight calling and Randy had flown off the handle. In fact, she had asked what was "going on" with Midnight before he asked if she'd called. "Shit," Joe said, starting to put it together. He looked over at Jessica. She had been watching him, and she could see that he had never even thought about how it might appear. It was very obvious that his love for his partner was indeed innocent, but obviously his wife had started to feel insecure about her place in his life. Hence the breakup.

When she looked at Joe again, he was shaking his head at her.

"What?" she said.

"I really need to get you made a detective."

They were both silent for the rest of the drive, and fifteen minutes later they were at the college. When Joe opened her door for her, as he had taken to doing, he surprised her by taking her hand to help her out. Then he pulled her to him and hugged her. "Thank you," he said, and Jessica felt very special.

Later in the day, as she watched him on the range, she realized she was indeed very jealous of Randy Sinclair. Joseph Michael Sinclair was the most incredible combination of tough and sensitive, and one hell of a gorgeous man to boot, and all Jessica could think was, Randy, you owe me a big one.

****

It was the middle of the following week when Joe called Midnight at home, and in her exhaustion she hadn't managed to be evasive enough when he asked how her academy training day had gone. She had replied, "Well, once I took Randy and her buddy into hand, everything was fine." Her voice conveyed the anger she still felt when she thought about the confrontation at the academy class. Dickerson had mentioned attempting more self-control next time, and Midnight had responding by telling him to shove it up his ass and followed up by telling him that perhaps he should teach his "girlfriend" and his sister to learn to keep their mouths shut.

"What happened?" Joe asked, sensing Midnight's instant hesitation. When she didn't reply, Joe grew angry and impatient at not being at home to keep an eye on things. "Damn it, Night, tell me."

"Joe," Midnight began, not wanting to tell him this on the phone, but knowing there was no way out of it now. "Jesus," she said, tears already starting in her eyes. Her voice reflected those tears. "It's Randy, Joe. God, I'm sorry, she's…" But she couldn't bring herself to tell him about Randy's new boyfriend.

Joe knew before Midnight even had to finish. He knew she would have called him immediately if Randy had been hurt, and he knew there was probably only one other thing that would make Midnight act the way she was. "She's screwin' him, isn't she?" Joe said. His voice sounded so far away, and Midnight just wanted to crawl through the phone line to try and cushion the pain she knew he was experiencing at that moment.

"Yeah," was all she could say, her voice a mere painful whisper.

Joe was silent for a long time, and Midnight suspected that tears were streaming from his eyes, but he wanted to hold on to some modicum of pride.

"You okay?" she asked finally, feeling nervous about his state of mind.

"Yeah." Joe's reply came in the same tone as her admission minutes before. "I gotta go, Night. I just… I gotta go." Joe hung up, and Midnight felt a stab of fear for her partner. She didn't know what he was going to do, but she waited over the next couple of days to hear from him. When he didn't call and he didn't answer her texts, she grew desperate. She called the Sacramento Police Department, identifying herself as a San Diego PD lieutenant and asking the dispatcher for Officer Jessica Harland's home number. Midnight was in her car and asked the dispatcher to transfer her. The dispatcher did as requested, but when Midnight got Jessica's house, Jessica's mother told her that Jessica was at the academy. Midnight explained that she was worried about her partner, Joe Sinclair, and that she needed to get ahold of Jessica to find out if he was okay. Martha Harland already had a soft spot for the man who had, as far as she was concerned, saved her daughter's life. She gave Midnight the cell number right away, indicating to Midnight that she herself hadn't seen Sergeant Sinclair over the last two days.

Midnight texted Jessica. When Jessica didn't answer, Midnight made a decision. She called the airlines and booked a flight for Sacramento. Before she left the office she texted Rick, and also texted Jessica again.

When her phone rang, she grabbed it. "Yeah?"

"You rang?" Rick said amiably.

"Yeah," Midnight said, looking at her watch as she drove. "Look, I need you to do me a big favor."

"And that would be?" Rick asked when she didn't continue.

"I need you to take Keyla for the weekend."

"I see," Rick replied, sounding irritated.

"Look." Midnight sighed. "Don't start with me, okay. I need you to do this. I have to go out of town, and Marie has the weekend off."

"Where is it you have to go?" Rick asked, still sounding irritated. Midnight could tell he thought she was going on some fling.

"I have to go to Sacramento, okay. Joe's up there and I can't get ahold of him, and…" She hesitated, sounding really concerned. "He's really screwed up right now."

Rick was silent for a moment. "You told him?" he asked, knowing there was only one thing that would send Joe into a tailspin at this point.

"I didn't mean to," Midnight said, "but hell, he would have found out eventually anyway. But now I can't get ahold of him, Rick." Her voice pleaded with him, and Rick couldn't help but feel for her at that moment. "If something's happened…" She trailed off, and he could almost see the tears in her eyes.

"He's alright, Midnight," Rick assured her. "And yeah, I'll take care of Keyla."

"Thanks," Midnight said, sounding relieved.

"Let me know how he is, okay?" Rick said. "I'll meet you at the house in a half hour."

They hung up, and Midnight reflected on the three of them. It was funny how when one of them was in real trouble, they could all put aside their own problems to help each other out. Cops were like that though, and the thought made Midnight feel a little stronger, just knowing that she could always rely on her friends when things were really bad. She realized then why Rick's infidelity had been so hard on her. It wasn't so much that he'd cheated, but that she had felt like she couldn't trust him anymore, couldn't count on him anymore. He was with an outsider now, and she couldn't expect him to drop everything when she or Joe needed him—maybe Sheila wouldn't understand, and maybe he'd decide to take her over them. Midnight pushed aside her train of thought as her car phone rang again.

This time it was Jessica.

"Lieutenant Chevalier?" She sounded uncertain; she hadn't been sure who was paging her, but she had hoped it had been Joe's partner.

"Yes, Jessica, it's me. Look, how's Joe? Have you seen him?"

"Thank God you called, Lieutenant. I don't know how he is, but I know it's not good. He was real quiet on Thursday, and then this morning he called me and told me he wasn't coming. He sounded really strange, so I went by the townhouse, and he was really bad off."

"He's been drinking," Midnight said.

"How'd you know?" Jessica asked, amazed.

"My partner has a propensity for drunken stupors when he's having a rough time. Right now it's really bad."

"It's his wife, isn't it?"

"I don't know how much he's told you…" Midnight started.

"She's cheating on him, isn't she?" It was more of a statement than a question.

"Yes, she is," Midnight replied, surprised that the girl seemed to know so much about Joe and his current problems. "Look, I'm coming up there. I should be there in about three hours. Can you keep an eye on him till then?"

"Yes, ma'am," Jessica replied, as if to a superior officer.

"And Jessica, Joe's a real mean drunk, and he…" She hesitated a little. "Well, he gets kind of violent sometimes, so watch it, okay?"

"Yes, ma'am," Jessica said, sounding less sure of herself.

"I'll see you when I get there."

"Okay."

Midnight hung up and continued on her way to her house to throw some things together. At home she had to explain to Mikeyla that she was going to stay with Daddy while she was gone, and that she had to go take care of Joe.

"What's wrong with Uncle Joe?" Mikeyla asked, sitting on her mother's lap.

Midnight wasn't sure what to say. Rick walked in the room and knelt down beside his daughter.

"Daddy!" Mikeyla squealed as she threw her arms around her father's neck. Then she looked up at him. "Daddy, what's wrong with Uncle Joe?"

Rick looked at Midnight, realizing this had been where he'd come in. Then he looked at his daughter and said, "His heart is hurting, baby, and Mommy has to go make sure that he gets better fast."

"Why does his heart hurt?"

"Well," Rick said, "you know how you feel when Mommy goes out of town, or how you felt when your cousins left?"

"Uh-huh," Mikeyla said, nodding.

"Well, Uncle Joe is missing someone right now, and it is making his heart hurt."

Mikeyla looked at Midnight. "And Mommy can make his heart stop hurting?"

"Yes, she can," Rick said, surprising Midnight with the surety of his statement. He looked at Midnight. "What time does your flight leave?"

"Whatever's next in line when I get there."

Rick looked at his watch. "You better get goin'. I'll close up things here."

"Thanks," Midnight told him for the second time that day. She leaned over and kissed Mikeyla. Grabbing up her overnight bag, she headed out the door.

Rick caught up to her a few minutes later. "Night!" he called, just as she was getting into her car.

"What?" she said hurriedly. But she stopped, seeing the concerned look on his face. "What is it?" she asked softly.

"Just..." Rick said, hesitating over the words. "Just be careful. I know what Joe can be like, and, well..." He trailed off, and Midnight knew he was thinking of the same incident she had been thinking of when she cautioned Jessica to be careful around Joe.

"I'll be careful," she assured him. Then she reached up and touched his face. He watched her intently. He wanted to kiss her, but he didn't want things to get complicated between them again; he was still recovering from their last night together and her subsequent rebuke the next day. Things were friendly between them now, and he wanted to keep it that way for the time being.

Midnight somehow seemed to understand what he was thinking, and, nodding as if they had just discussed it, she got in her car. Rick watched as she drove off. Then he turned and walked back to the house. He had decided to stay there with Mikeyla rather than having to drag her somewhere strange. He walked inside and closed the door.

Midnight drove down the Sacramento freeway, her mind on nothing but reaching Joe's townhouse. After a few minutes she found the address and walked up to the front door. She was wearing her usual jeans, boots, and a black cotton shirt that was open at the neck. Over it she had thrown Rick's jean jacket, which she had found in her car; obviously she had forgotten to return it to him. If felt a little like home to her. At the front door, she knocked, looking the door's hardware over as she waited, in case she needed to kick it in. She grinned to herself. Yeah, that'd look real good, she thought wryly, having to kick in my second's door in case he's passed out.

The door opened, and Midnight found herself facing a young woman a little taller than herself with auburn hair and green eyes. The woman seemed taken aback by Midnight's appearance, but she smiled warmly at the leader of FORS all the same.

"Lieutenant Chevalier?" Jessica asked, knowing it was a dumb question. She had been shocked at how young Midnight looked—she'd also expected someone... bigger, was the only word she could think of, as she stepped aside to let Midnight in.

"That's something I've been meaning to mention," Midnight said as she looked around. "It's Midnight, not Lieutenant." She extended her hand and Jessica took it. "Now," Midnight said, "where is my ailing partner?"

"In the kitchen. He's been drinking all day, from what I can tell." Midnight nodded and headed in the direction Jessica had indicated. Jessica followed along behind, not sure what to do.

When Midnight walked in the kitchen, Joe's head was down on his arms as they rested on the table. He hadn't shaved in going on three days, and he looked like hell, from what Midnight could see. But she had expected no different. Joe lifted his head, as if sensing her there, and Midnight's eyes filled instantly with tears at the look of loss in his eyes.

"Night?" Joe said, as if not believing his eyes. Midnight moved to him, kneeling down beside him. Joe turned in the chair and pulled her up into an embrace. They were both in tears. After a few moments, Midnight pulled away, standing and drawing Joe to his feet.

"Bedroom?" she asked, looking at Jessica, who had been watching with interest. She pointed to the hallway. Midnight nodded. She reached out and took Joe's hand, leading him almost like a child to the bedroom. Joe stood watching as she sat down on the bed; she moved a few pillows, then grabbed his hand and pulled him down.

Jessica took the chance to wander down the hallway and, noting that the bedroom door was still open, looked into the room. Joe's head rested on Midnight's lap, and his body was stretched out across the bed, both arms basically wrapped around Midnight's midsection. Midnight rested her head against the headboard, her eyes alternating from staring up at the ceiling to looking down at Joe. Joe was either passed out or asleep—Jessica wasn't sure which—and Midnight was stroking his mane of dirty-blond hair.

Jessica could see that she had been right in wanting Midnight to be here to take care of Joe. It amazed her still how much she had come to care about this man, in such a short time. When she had talked to Joe and he had sounded so despondent, she had been almost sick with worry. By comparison, she had been very relieved when Midnight told her she was coming up. Now, watching Midnight with him, Jessica found herself wishing she could have such a close relationship with someone as fantastic as she had come to feel Joe was. Jessica could also see the problem that Randy was having with the friendship—it was difficult to discern where the "lovers" stopped and the "friendship" started between the two of them.

Midnight glanced up, noticing Jessica standing in the doorway. She smiled at the younger woman.

"Is he going to be okay?" Jessica asked.

Midnight looked down at her sleeping partner, and then back at Jessica. "Eventually," she said, sighing. "This is just really rough on him. You have to understand," she said very seriously, "Randy means everything to him, and to have her do this... Well, it's like she's taking everything from him and kicking him on the way out."

Jessica nodded, understanding what Midnight was saying. Then she looked at Joe for a long moment and shook her head. "Why would she want to give him up?"

Midnight smiled. She'd heard that tone before, from other women who thought Randy an incredibly lucky woman. "You know the old saying, the grass is always greener. Randy thinks she wants to be independent. You see, Joe met her when she was still very young and very innocent." Midnight's emphasis was on "innocent." Jessica took her meaning, surprised all the same. "Anyway," Midnight continued, "I don't think she realizes how lucky she's really been. I know Joe can be a real pain in the ass sometimes when it comes to overprotectiveness, but I also know that he can be reasoned with." She paused, looking sad. "And what that dumb kid doesn't seem to understand is that it doesn't have to be all or nothing—she just has to try to talk to him. But she didn't want to do that, she wanted to run away and be free." Midnight's voice grew angry on the last sentence.

Jessica was quiet for a few minutes, not sure if she should tell Midnight what she had told Joe a few days before. Finally she took a deep breath and said it. "Do you think their breakup had anything to do with you and Joe's relationship?"

Midnight looked at the other woman for a long moment, surprised that she had been brave enough to say it, for one, and two, for thinking along the same lines Midnight had been over the past couple of weeks. "You know, a conversation that Randy and I had a few weeks back has started to come back to me again and again. Randy was pissed when I told her that if she really wanted to be a police officer, she might have to give up some things to make it happen. She wanted to know what I'd given up, and one of the things I listed was Joe." Midnight shook her head. "I thought about it later and thought that maybe I shouldn't have said it in quite that way, that maybe she thinks that I still wanted him, but that wasn't the point I was trying to make. Moot point now though, huh?"

Midnight seemed to be looking to her to validate her thinking, and Jessica felt good to know that Midnight already liked her enough to at least ask for her opinion. "Maybe," was all she said at first. Then, wanting to be helpful if she could, she continued. "Or maybe Randy wanted it to mean something else. Maybe that's the only way she thinks she can make a break with him, you know, trying to get out without being the one burned."

Midnight considered that for a long moment, wanting Jessica to be right, wanting to be absolved of being the cause of Joe and Randy's breakup. The thought of it had been weighing heavy on her heart for the last few weeks. "Maybe," she said finally. "Randy does seem to be spoiling for a fight."

"Fight?" Jessica asked.

Midnight was thinking back. She nodded absently, but when she noticed Jessica was waiting for an explanation, she grinned. "Sorry. Yeah, she and this friend of hers have been trying to pick a fight with me. They came to my office once, right after your accident, and then they started shit with me when I did a class for them at the academy."

"Started shit how?"

"Just being stupid. They tried to say that I probably couldn't handle an actual physical confrontation with a gang member, since I just sat behind a desk and all." Jessica was already grinning by the time Midnight finished.

"I take it you put them back in their place?" Jessica said, having heard about Midnight from Joe and knowing she wouldn't stand for that kind of insult.

"You'd be right," Midnight said, her face indicating the pleasure she had taken in doing so.

"Well, I'd say Randy was wanting to find fault with him then," Jessica said, nodding at Joe's sleeping form.

"Yeah, maybe."

They were silent for a few minutes, both of them watching the man they were discussing sleep on.

Midnight looked up at Jessica. "Have you ever considered investigations?"

Jessica began to laugh. "Your partner asked me the exact same thing. You two are almost like a married couple—you've been together so long, you think alike."

"Yeah, tell me about it," Midnight said, rolling her eyes. "Know how hard that makes it to keep anything from the guy?"

"I'd imagine pretty hard."

Midnight and Jessica talked for a few more minutes, then Midnight suggested that Jessica head home. She promised to call her the next day to let her know how Joe was doing. Jessica left.

Midnight was dozing when she felt Joe begin to move around. She woke to find him watching her.

"Hey," she said, noting that he looked a lot more sober now.

"Hey," Joe replied. Then his face grew serious. "Tell me everything," he said, his tone resigned.

Midnight shook her head. "Like hell I will. I'm not into turning the knife once it's in."

"Night, I need to know," Joe said, his voice taking on an angry edge.

"What d'ya want to know, Joe?" she asked harshly. "You want to know if they're fucking, or do you want to know if they're doing it in public?"

Joe closed his eyes, visibly flinching from her words. He shook his head slowly as he sat up. "I can't do this, Night," he said, his tone all but dead. "I can't take it."

"Well, you're not going to take it, Joe." Midnight knew she had to snap him out of his depression fast. She recognized the look in his eyes and the tone of his voice. It was like when his aunt had accused him of killing his own parents. Joe had been devastated, and it had not only just about killed him, but had gotten very violent where Midnight was concerned as well. "You're going to divorce the fucking bitch and move on. That's what she's doing."

Joe was shaking his head, as if trying to keep out her words. "No, I can't," he said, with so much pain in his voice there were tears in Midnight's eyes a split second later. "I can't, Night."

"Yes, you can!" Midnight yelled. "Damn it, Joe, she doesn't deserve you, if she can do this to you." She was crying now, and Joe turned to look at her. He had heard the anger and hurt in her voice. She looked at him, her eyes staring straight into his soul. "If they can do this to us," she said, so quietly Joe felt it more than heard it.

He pulled her into his arms, holding her close to him. As she cried, he realized he'd been remiss in taking care of her during this thing with Rick. She had seemed okay, and he had his own problems, so he had just let it go. He knew now that she hadn't been okay, and he knew that Randy cheating on him had only polarized the whole thing with Rick for her.

He sat holding her for a long time, until her cries quieted and she just rested against him. "Joe," she said, her voice muffled by his shirt.

"What?" he asked, trying to look at her, but she kept her face in his shirt.

"I have to tell you something, but it can't go any farther than this room." She still wouldn't look at him, and Joe began to feel a cold, hard knot in his stomach. It was a rare time when Midnight wouldn't look him in the eye.

"Tell me," he said quietly.

"I'm pregnant," she said, so simply that Joe wasn't sure he had heard her correctly.

"You're what?"

"You heard me right the first time—pregnant," Midnight said, deadly quiet.

Joe was silent for a while, trying to digest what she had just said. He knew this news wasn't as simple as it sounded. Midnight's pregnancy with Mikeyla had been very difficult, the labor almost costing her life. The doctors had more or less told her not to have any more children, saying that her body just wasn't designed for the stress of a full-term pregnancy and definitely not for the trauma of a labor and birth. Joe figured that Midnight's hesitation in telling him stemmed from the difficult idea of having to have an abortion.

"Night," he started, trying not to sound too callous, "if you want me to go with you, to be there, if you don't want Rick, but—"

Midnight cut him off. "I'm having it."

Joe almost stopped breathing. "Night," he began, but she cut him off again.

"Don't, Joe. Don't tell me I can't, because I can, and I'm going to." Her voice was determined, but she still didn't look at him.

"How far along are you?" Joe asked, wondering if it was already too late to terminate the pregnancy safely, and that was why she'd been afraid to tell him.

"About ten weeks," Midnight said, feeling Joe relax instantly. "It doesn't matter, Joe. I'm not getting rid of this baby."

Joe reflected on it, realizing how this would sound to any outsider, but he knew the baby was Rick's because he knew that contrary to what Rick thought, Midnight hadn't slept with anyone but him for over four years. Certainly not with Griff, not while she was still legally married to Rick.

"Obviously you haven't told Rick," Joe said disapprovingly.

"No," Midnight said, bringing her head up sharply to look at him. "And if you tell him, I swear to God, I'll kill you." Her voice was deadly serious, and Joe didn't doubt her for a minute. Midnight knew that if Rick knew about the baby, he would either make an extensive effort to talk her out of having it or he'd stay with her just to make sure she was alright.

Joe looked at her for a long time. He could see the determination in her eyes, and he knew he'd be wasting his breath if he tried to talk her out of her course of action. "Fine then," he said finally, in a way that brooked no argument. "As soon as I get back from here, you and Mikeyla are moving in with me." His tone sharpened further as he saw Midnight begin to shake her head. "Don't fucking shake your head at me. If you're stupid enough to put yourself in this much danger, then you're damn well going to be smart enough to take my help!" He was angry now. The idea of Midnight going through something this dangerous alone was not only unbearable, but unimaginable.

Midnight stared at him for a long moment, then started to grin. "Jesus," she said finally. "I'm surprised you didn't propose while you were at it."

"Fuck you," Joe replied, smiling. "Maybe I just haven't gotten to that part yet."

Midnight reached out, touching his face tenderly. "Don't tease me, Joseph Michael Sinclair, I just might think you're serious." Her grin was reckless, and Joe knew what was about to happen. Midnight's hand trailed up his neck to entwine itself in his hair, and with confidence born of complete comfort with the man she was with, she pulled him toward her, her lips meeting his in a kiss that left them both breathless minutes later.

When they parted, Joe could see the fire burning in his partner's eyes, and he knew it was a mixture of passion and a desire for revenge. It was a dangerous combination, and Joe knew it would be so easy to give in and let their bodies lead them down very familiar territory. To make love, and feel so close to each other again, to feel connected and united against all enemies again. For a few moments, Joe fought

47

it. He wanted to tell her they had to stop; he even started to say the words, but looking into her eyes, it just didn't make sense to say no.

Randy was gone, Rick was gone—what else was there for them? Why didn't they deserve each other again? They were the ones who had been faithful, the ones who had waited and watched. Who'd backed each other up, who'd fought every war together, against all odds.

He felt almost relieved to give in and take his partner in his arms again. Bringing his lips down to meet hers, they melted together. His hands traveled down her body, and Midnight responded by lying back on the bed, pulling him down with her. Joe's body covering hers, his weight on her, was so familiar, and Midnight grasped the feeling with both hands, wanting to cling to him as if she were drowning.

Hours later, they lay on the bed together. Joe held her the way he had so many times before. They didn't talk about what they had just done; they both knew it would hurt the respective people in their lives. Good! they both thought, at about the same time.

The next morning, after a nice extra few hours of sleep that both of them had needed badly, Midnight and Joe sat together at his kitchen table, drinking coffee and talking.

"Are you sure you're ready to have me and Keyla at your house?" Midnight said skeptically.

"Yes, I'm sure," Joe assured her.

"You have no idea what it's like to live with a two-year-old."

"I've lived with you, haven't I?" Joe replied, a grin on his face.

Midnight rolled her eyes at him, smiling. "I walked right into that one, didn't I?"

"Basically."

And so the morning went. At around noon, Midnight called Jessica to let her know Joe was alright and that everything was going to be okay.

"You're sure?" Jessica asked, remembering how badly off Joe had been the night before and not believing that he was fine just over eighteen hours later.

"Come and see him if you don't believe me," Midnight said, smiling. Joe walked into the bedroom and looked at her quizzically.

"She doesn't believe it?" he asked, loudly enough for Jessica to hear. "Too damn young to be that cynical already." He walked over to the opposite side of the bed from where Midnight sat and lay down across it, his head next to her. Flipping over on his back, he reached up and took the phone from his partner.

"Look here, young lady," he said, his smile wide, "don't you doubt my partner. She's a decorated peace officer, after all."

"Well," Jessica replied, laughing, "you do sound a lot better."

"But you're still not convinced?" Joe was still grinning. "Fine then, come over here and I'll take you two ladies to lunch. Will that convince you?"

"Maybe," Jessica said.

"Fine." Joe looked at his watch. "It's ten past twelve now. Be here by... oh, one thirty."

"Yes, sir!" Jessica replied crisply. Then she laughed again. "See you two then." She hung up, and found herself happy to be included—also, quite interested in how they acted when they were together.

Joe rested his cheek on Midnight's legs for a minute, having had to stretch past her to hang up the phone. Midnight caressed his face, almost out of habit.

"Lunch, huh?" she said, smiling down at him, even though he was facing the floor with his chin on her thigh.

"Yeah. There's a place downtown I want to take you to."

"Called?"

"Called The Distillery. They have really good steak sandwiches—Jess took me there."

"She's a good kid," Midnight said.

Joe nodded. "Yeah, quick as hell too."

Midnight knew what Joe meant. "Tell me," she said, "did she tell you her theory about Randy?"

"Yeah." Joe shook his head, as if he couldn't understand Randy's thinking, but then looked guilty right behind that. "Oops." He had remembered that Randy was right, now that he had slept with Midnight.

Midnight had followed the line of Joe's thoughts easily, and she shook her head. "Hey, she wasn't right about it. The timing makes a big difference here, you know."

"Yeah, I know," Joe said. He turned over to look at her. "How 'bout you?" he asked, and she knew what he meant.

"Fuck him," she said, her eyes devoid of shame.

Joe looked at her for a long time, trying to decide if she really meant it. "Night," he said finally, his eyes showing concern for her emotional state. "Really, how's this gonna be on you?" It was a good question; they had never slept together when either or both of them were in love with someone else. It was only logical that this time would be different, and that it might be harder for one or both of them.

Midnight stared at the wall for a long moment, thinking about the question. She lay back on the bed, blowing her breath out in a sigh. "I don't know," was all she said.

Joe sat up, looking down at her lying there. "It's gotta be worth it," he said softly. "I mean, if it's going to cause us more grief than it would being apart…"

Midnight looked over at him. "I need you right now, and I'd say it's a safe bet that you need me too. Isn't that what we're about?"

"Yeah, it is." Joe knew she was right, but also that it wasn't as simple as that anymore. He understood her though, and he knew she was aware of the hazards they were negotiating this time—and that he didn't need to point any of them out to her. Joe had enough respect for his longtime partner to trust her. She knew what they were playing against, and he didn't need to put her in the position of having to consider each obstacle out loud.

Later that day, Jessica arrived, and she was very obviously relieved at Joe's transformed appearance. He looked even better than he had originally, and something about that made Jessica curious, but she didn't see anything obvious in the way they were acting. Midnight and Joe's union was different this time; it was based more on the need to be united than the actual act of being together. They were close during the day—in the car, Joe would put his hand on the edge of the seat next to Midnight's leg, and after a few minutes, Midnight's hand would rest on top of his—but there were no long, passionate kisses in public, no real intimate contact at all. Jessica wasn't sure if this was just their normal behavior or if something had happened between them. After lunch, Joe insisted on taking Midnight over to meet Jessica's family.

Martha remembered Midnight from their phone call, when Midnight had been trying to get ahold of Jessica. "I see you found him," she said, patting Joe on the shoulder.

"I never can hide for long," Joe said, smiling.

"Especially since tequila bottles are clear." Midnight's eyes glittered with humor.

"She told you," James said, laughing.

"She does often," Joe said, widening his eyes at his partner as if she had told them something she wasn't supposed to. Midnight just grinned.

"Well," Gerald Harland said, giving Midnight an approving stare, "it's no wonder he's such a good guy then, with a partner to keep him in line."

"I do my best." Midnight smiled winningly at the older man.

They had all talked for a while, sitting comfortably in the family room of the large, spacious house. Gary had again cornered Joe alone as soon as he got the chance.

"You have a partner that looks like that," Gary said, shaking his head in disbelief, "and you married someone else? Are you fucking nuts, or what?" Joe could hear the humor in the younger man's voice.

"I asked," Joe said with a conspiratorial smile, "but she turned me down."

"Well, that's because she was waiting for me," Gary said, pretending to preen.

"Oh yeah, I'll just bet, junior. She's only about eight years older than you."

"No way," Gary said, genuinely surprised.

"Yes way," Joe replied. "Besides, she'd chew you up and spit you out—that's what she does with young pups like you."

"Well, I'd sure die happy, wouldn't I?" Gary smiled wistfully. He and Joe rejoined the group, still laughing.

"What?" Jessica asked, eyeing the two men suspiciously. She could tell her brother was already all cow-eyed about Midnight.

"Nothin'," Joe said, trying to keep the smile off his face. He winked at Midnight when she looked over at him, and her eyes narrowed but she had a slight grin on her face.

By the time they left the Harlands' home, after being basically held hostage until they accepted an invitation to stay for dinner, Midnight was very happy she had come.

"They're really nice people," she said, a melancholy look on her face.

"Yeah," Joe said, seeing her expression. "Kind of family it'd be nice to have, huh?"

"Yeah," Midnight answered, the look in her eyes backing up the affirmation.

Joe and Midnight spent most of the next afternoon relaxing at his townhouse, watching TV and lying on the couch or the floor. They went out to dinner that evening, choosing a nice, quiet, unassuming Basque restaurant called The Sheepherder's Inn. They ate and talked late into the evening, everyone around them assuming they were a couple. Midnight decided to stay the next day, telling Joe she wanted to see his academy class.

Monday served as a better indication to Jessica that something was different between them from when Midnight had arrived on Friday night. Midnight and Joe drove over to pick her up, and Jessica was surprised when she saw that Midnight was driving. She looked at Joe quizzically as he held open the door for her.

"She pulled rank," he said in answer to her unasked question, and Jessica smiled.

"Oh. Good morning, Midnight." Jessica smiled at the other woman from the back seat.

"Hey," Midnight said, returning the smile.

They talked all the way to the college, with Joe teasing Midnight about the music she insisted on listening to.

"She's into the dancier stuff," he explained to Jessica.

"Yeah," Midnight said, "not that morbid crap you like to listen to." But her smile softened the words.

"Not everything in life is a party, dear love," Joe said, returning her smile.

"Ah, indeed."

Jessica asked Midnight about her police background and how she had gotten started.

"It was either that or I would have ended up in jail, or dead," Midnight said, her fingers drumming on the steering wheel to the beat of Ace of Base's "All That She Wants."

"You were a gang member too?" Jessica said. She knew she shouldn't be surprised, but she was all the same.

"Oh yeah," Midnight said, grinning at Joe.

"How old were you when you quit?" Jessica asked.

"Eighteen," Midnight said, and Joe saw the shadow cross her face.

"And why did you quit?" Jessica asked, right as Joe turned to shake his head at her, but the question was already out.

Midnight caught Joe's movement and put her hand out to touch his leg, trying to tell him it was okay. She looked at Jessica in the rearview mirror. "My little brother was killed in a gang fight."

"Oh," Jessica said. "I'm sorry."

Midnight shook her head. "It's okay."

They arrived at the academy, and Joe introduced his "boss" to the students. Midnight had just planned to watch them as they conducted their normal class, but everyone seemed to have questions for her.

"You're a lieutenant?" one girl asked, respect clear in her voice.

"Yep," Midnight said, "but believe me, it ain't all it's cracked up to be."

"Do you have to have a four-year degree to be a lieutenant?" the same woman asked. She obviously wanted to become one herself one day.

"You don't have to, but I do, and I don't think it hurt."

"What's your degree in?" one of the young men asked.

"I have a bachelor's in psychology and a law degree."

"Wow!" A lot of the students seemed impressed.

"So why don't you practice law instead of being a police officer?" another man asked. "I mean, wouldn't there be more money in being a lawyer?"

Midnight considered the question for a moment. "I love my job, and money's not a real big thing for me."

"You're not rich like the sergeant, are you?" someone in the back asked, starting a low chuckle around the class.

"Nope," Midnight replied, catching Joe's eyes. The truth was, being married to Rick did make her what most people would consider well-off, but she wasn't considering Rick's family's money as her own.

Another of the women spoke up. "Do you have to get into fights with gang members?"

"Yes, I do."

"Even as a lieutenant?" the young lady wanting to become a lieutenant asked, obviously worried about the prospect in her future. Some of the others laughed.

Midnight laughed as well. "Well, it's not a job requirement. I could just stay in my office and take it easy, but I prefer to get down and dirty with the rest of 'em."

"Could you show us some of your hand-to-hand stuff?" asked one of the women eagerly.

Midnight started to nod, but Joe said, "No."

Midnight looked over at him. "Yes, I can."

"I don't think it's a good idea," Joe said, narrowing his eyes at her.

"Well, I do," Midnight replied, her eyes returning the challenge.

The class waited in silence, watching their exchange.

Joe looked at his students. "Excuse us for just a minute." He took Midnight gently by the arm and walked over to the far wall of the outdoor range.

"What're you doing?" he said, his voice a harsh whisper.

"What?" Midnight replied, purposely obtuse.

"Don't you think you should take it easy?"

Midnight snorted. "I was flippin' your wife over my shoulder a week ago, and she was gunnin' for me. I think I can handle this."

Joe's lips tightened at the mention of Randy's behavior the week before. After a few moments he said, "Fine."

They walked back over to the class, and Midnight proceeded to demonstrate some hand-to-hand combat moves. It was obvious to Joe that she had no intention of taking it easy—she might have decided to have Rick's baby, but she wasn't going to let it break her stride.

That afternoon, on the drive home from the academy, Joe noticed that Midnight was moving her wrist rather stiffly. She caught his eye and saw the sardonic twist to his lips.

"What?" she asked.

"Hurt your wrist, didn't you?" he said, sounding smug.

Midnight made a face at him. "Okay, yeah, I did—so?" She shrugged. "That last guy weighed more than I thought, no biggy."

"I guess asking his weight would have been out of the question."

"Yes, when I'm telling these kids that weight and size don't matter," she chided. "And is it me, or are these candidates getting younger and younger every day?"

Joe laughed. "It's you," he said, his grin wide. "And me—we're getting old."

"Great," Midnight said, leaning back against the seat.

Jessica was sitting in the back seat, listening to their banter. She couldn't picture either of them as "old."

"Yeah," Joe said, grinning, "you should have heard that one giving me a hard time about my age." He had jabbed his thumb in Jessica's direction on the word "that."

"Ooh," Midnight said, smiling and glancing over the headrest at Jessica. "Brutal."

"Yeah," Jessica said, "but you're not as... well, I mean, you're younger than that." She had pulled herself up short from saying old, but Joe and Midnight knew what she had started to say and they both laughed.

"Oh, yeah, I'm younger than him by, what..." She looked at Joe, as if trying to remember. "At least a year and a half."

Jessica started coughing like she was choking, her eyes bugging out at Midnight. "No way!"

"Oh yes," Midnight assured her.

Before Jessica could reply there was a sharp beeping noise. Joe glanced over at Midnight, and she looked down. She unclipped her cell from her belt and checked the number. She looked up at Joe, all humor gone from her face. She turned the phone so he could see. All texts from FORS included the members' two-digit police radio call numbers, so that Midnight would know who it was. The number the phone displayed now was two-two—Rick's.

"Shit," Joe said, shaking his head. He blew his breath out in a frustrated sigh.

"I told him I'd call him to tell him how you were—I totally forgot." Midnight was shaking her head too. And Jessica knew it was Midnight's husband that had texted her. It was obvious that Midnight was reluctant to talk to him, and the grave look on Joe's face told Jessica everything that she had suspected was true. She sat silently in the back seat, not wanting to intrude or eavesdrop—although it was physically impossible not to—but hoping they wouldn't feel uncomfortable with her there.

"What should I do?" Midnight asked Joe, watching him closely. They had known they would have to deal with this part of their decision, but they hadn't expected to this soon.

"If you don't call, he's just gonna get more worried, and probably more pissed," Joe said, reaching into his jacket pocket and pulling out his cellular phone. He handed it to her, his face still showing the conflict going on inside him. Rick was his best friend, and now, by all rights, he had slept with Rick's wife. Joe was starting to feel the discomfort of being the other man, a place he'd never been in before.

Midnight took the phone and dialed. Joe's phone had a hands-free option, but she figured the less Joe had to hear, the better. Midnight knew the private hell Joe was going through; she knew his loyalty to Rick ran very deep, and that right now Joe was feeling like he had betrayed his best friend. And no matter what the circumstances were, he had—they had.

"'Lo," Rick answered, expecting it to be her.

"Hi, it's me," Midnight said, all color gone from her voice at hearing Rick.

"Well, you sound chipper," he said, sounding worried.

"Just been a long day. Sorry I didn't call you sooner, but I've been a little busy." She took a breath, feeling like she was talking too much and too fast. "Anyway, Joe's fine."

"He is," Rick said, more of a statement than a question. He sounded suspicious, and Midnight was more sure than ever that her husband was part bloodhound. He could smell fear, even over four hundred miles away.

"Yeah, he's okay now," Midnight said, not sure what else to say without out and out lying to him, which she couldn't and wouldn't do.

Rick was silent for a moment. "What's goin' on?" he asked, and Midnight closed her eyes. Joe saw her face, and he knew that Rick knew what had happened. Midnight opened her eyes and looked at Joe. His lips twitched as he saw the pain in her eyes. He knew this was hard for her; it was for him too.

"Whaddya mean?" she said, trying to stave him off.

"Don't even fucking try it with me, Midnight," Rick said, angry now.

"Try what—what are you talking about?"

"I don't believe this!"

Midnight knew he hadn't even heard her last question. "What is it you don't believe?" she said, finally feeling her own anger start to burn.

"You're sleeping with him again, aren't you?" Rick said, as if he didn't believe his own question.

"What makes you say that?" Midnight said, starting to dig her heels in. Joe looked over and saw that her eyes were flashing green fire now. He knew that was how she was going to get through this.

"Don't even try to lie to me, Midnight. I know you, and I know him." His voice made "him" sound like a cuss word. "Was that the plan all along?" he said, his anger turning to cold rage.

"You don't know what you're talking about," Midnight said, her voice low, but her anger simmering just below the surface.

"Don't I?" Rick said, nasty now. "Is that why Joe ran his own wife off, so you two could get back in bed together?" His voice grated against her ear, and Midnight had to fight to control the naked anger she was feeling.

"You sonofabitch, you have a lot of fucking nerve passing judgement on me or Joe, considering your current score card!"

"Yeah, well at least I didn't fuck Joe's wife!"

"No," Midnight yelled, "you fucked a total stranger. I guess that's much better. Go to hell, Rick!" She jammed her finger down on the END button and threw the phone onto the floor of the car. Her eyes burned with angry tears, and Joe reached out to grip her balled-up fist.

"Well, that was nice," he said into the silence, his voice indicating that it was anything but.

"What was I supposed to do?" Midnight said, still angry.

"Whoa!" Joe held up a hand in a defensive gesture. "I'm not saying you were outta line."

Midnight's cell went off again, and she knew it was Rick. She yanked the phone off her belt, made a point of turning it off, and threw it on the floor. Midnight and Joe exchanged a look. They had both known it would come down to this, but they just hadn't been ready for it yet.

There was silence in the car for a few minutes. Midnight and Joe didn't want to talk, and Jessica knew she should say nothing. Both Joe and Midnight were surprised when Joe's cellular phone rang, and they looked at each other; they knew it was Rick. Joe could turn the phone off, but it would just be putting off the inevitable. Midnight leaned down and picked up the cell, handing it to Joe. He switched the phone to hands-free and set it on the dashboard, depressing the SEND button to answer the call.

"Yeah?" Joe said, his voice low.

"Joe." Rick said the name as if it were foreign to him, and Joe could feel his anger pulsing through the line. "I need to speak to my wife." He emphasized the last two words.

"She's sittin' right here," Joe replied, not allowing any apology into his voice.

"Midnight," Rick said, obviously realizing that he was on speaker now. "I want custody of Mikeyla."

Midnight guffawed. "I don't think so."

"I have a right to spend time with her," Rick said, anger in his voice again. Midnight had no way of knowing that when she had hung up on him, he had sat in his car, gasping for breath at the sharp pain her admitted betrayal had caused. His eyes had filled with angry tears, and he had wanted nothing more than to kill his "best friend" at that moment.

"You are spending time with her," Midnight said, "right now."

"Yeah, while you're up there fucking my best friend!" Rick shouted, his voice breaking on the last two words.

"Don't bring Mikeyla into this," Joe put in, because Midnight had winced at the pain his words had just caused her. She had felt like he'd just stuck a knife in her heart.

"Fuck you, Joe. She's my daughter, and you should just stay the hell out of it, and my marriage!" Rick's anger burned in Joe's ears, and he knew they were in dangerous territory now.

"Seems like I'm in the middle of it now, doesn't it?" Joe said, his voice frustratingly calm, although the look on his face belied the pain his betrayal was costing him.

"Yeah, so it would seem," Rick replied, deadly quiet.

"Look," Midnight said, having recovered her composure. "You can't have her, and that's final."

"And who the fuck are you?" Rick blazed at her. "The judge and jury?"

"No," Midnight said, trying to remain calm. This was her daughter she was fighting for now. "I'm her mother, and you won't get her."

"Like hell I won't," Rick said, his voice deceptively calm now.

"Damn it, Rick, don't do this!" Joe said, aware of the agony his threat was causing Midnight, especially with the knowledge that she was carrying Rick's baby.

"Stay out of it, Joe, I'm warnin' you." Rick sounded like a gang member, his voice pure ice.

"Yeah?" Joe said. "Bring it on, but don't hide behind a little girl."

"Oh, you and I aren't done, believe me," Rick said dangerously.

"Anytime," Joe replied, his jaw set in a hard line. Midnight was looking at him, her expression indicating her protest at their exchange.

"Let's keep this on an even keel, okay?" she said, trying to break the direction of their conversation.

"Fine," Rick said after a moment, obviously not done, "but I will be suing you for custody, so you better be ready to give her up." His voice was cold now, and Midnight knew he was serious.

"Over my dead body," she said, just as coldly.

"I could be so lucky," Rick shot back, sounding very serious. Then he slammed the phone down, breaking the connection.

Midnight stared at the phone on the dashboard as if it were a snake. It was obvious that she had been shocked at Rick's words.

Joe looked at her. She was deathly pale, clearly devastated at what Rick had said. Joe knew he was serious about suing her for custody of Mikeyla.

"What if he does it?" Midnight said after a long silence. "What if he takes her?" There were tears in her voice now, and Joe wanted to throttle Rick.

"Won't happen," he said simply. Midnight looked up at him, her eyes shining with her tears, begging him to be right. Joe shrugged. "Fact of the matter is, I have more money than him, and I'll spend it all to keep him from taking your daughter."

"Yeah," Midnight said, looking very tired all of a sudden. "Maybe you can use your current lawyer—you know, Rick's father." Her voice was strident, as if she knew it was hopeless.

"I don't think even Robert would back him on this," Joe said, surprising Midnight.

"Why not?"

"Let's just say that they aren't exactly fond of Sheila Theland."

"And why's that?" Midnight remembered what Deborah had said about Rick "dodging" that one.

Joe looked over at his partner, as if measuring how much he should tell her. But he wasn't exactly feeling loyal to Rick at that moment. "She tried to trap him into marrying her."

"I see," Midnight said, thinking it said a lot about how much Rick wanted to get away from her if he'd go to a woman who had done that. She shook her head, not understanding how their lives had gotten so far off track again. The rest of the ride was made in silence.

When Joe dropped Jessica off at her home, he made a point of getting out of the car and walking her to the door.

"I'm sorry," he said. "I know you probably just heard a lot more than you ever wanted to know about Midnight and me and Rick…" He trailed off as Jessica shook her head, her eyes sad.

"I'm sorry you're all going through this," she said, placing her hand on his arm. She looked back at Midnight, sitting with her head against the headrest, her eyes closed. "I hope everything turns out okay." She reached up to kiss Joe on the cheek, then whispered, "You take care of her, and yourself."

Joe looked down at her. He realized she was a pretty special young lady, and he found himself very glad to know her.

"Thanks," he said, his eyes indicating the appreciation he felt for her understanding. He reached out and hugged her, kissing the top of her head. "You're a good kid." Jessica felt warmed by the words. She smiled up at him, then turned and walked into her parents' home.

Joe walked back to the car, and they drove back to his town-house.

That night Midnight and Joe spent the evening quietly. Midnight was very disturbed by the conversations with Rick. She told Joe that she didn't want them coming to blows over her.

Joe looked at her for a long moment, raising an eyebrow. "It won't be the first time," he said.

"I know, but I don't want it to happen." She said it very seriously, but Joe shook his head.

"Midnight, the minute we kissed again, it became inevitable that Rick and I would get into it over you." Then he looked at her, his eyes piercing hers. "You didn't actually think he'd let my sleeping with you go, did you?" He saw the look in her eyes and started shaking his head in disbelief. "God, you really are screwed up right now. Midnight, you haven't really convinced yourself that he doesn't love you, have you?"

"Yeah, I can really tell right now," Midnight said, sounding hurt.

"Jesus, Night, you don't really know him, do you? He wouldn't be doing all this, stayin' where he is, if he didn't love you. Night, if he didn't love you, he would have been gone a long time ago. I can't believe you don't know that." He wasn't sure why he was telling her this, but he knew that what he was saying was true. He knew Rick wanted to kill him right now, and if he'd been in the same town they'd probably be doing some serious damage to each other at that moment. Joe wouldn't have been concerned about his relationship with Midnight if he didn't know that his best friend still loved her.

Midnight was looking at him now, her eyes narrowed, and he knew he hadn't convinced her. "He is gone, Joe, or don't you consider him moving in with that bitch as gone?"

Joe shook his head. "He ain't gone. Shit, Midnight, he still works for you. He's still in the same town. I mean, he managed to get you pregnant even in the middle of all of this—you think that's gone? I think you need to look the word up."

Midnight got up from his couch and walked into the other room, obviously not ready to accept any of what he was saying. He gave up for the time being.

Later that night, he slid into bed next to her. She was lying on her side, but he could tell she wasn't sleeping. He reached out, pulling her back against him and wrapping his arms around her protectively. Midnight relaxed against him.

"What's going to happen, Joe?" she said quietly. "What's he going to do when he finds out I'm pregnant?"

Joe was silent for a long time, not sure what to tell her. He knew Rick would assume it was his at first, and that he would really come after him—but also that it would almost be better for Midnight if Rick thought the baby was Joe's. Rick would put her through hell if he knew she was carrying his child. He would push for a reconciliation, and Joe knew Midnight would never take him back on those terms, and that it could really be the end for Midnight and Rick. Joe realized that no matter what Midnight meant to him, or what he meant to her, they were meant for other people and no amount of carrying on would change that. For now they were together, and Joe would do anything within his power to keep Rick from hurting her anymore.

As if she had read his thoughts, Midnight turned over to look at him. "You're going to let him think it's yours, aren't you?" she said, her eyes holding fear.

Joe looked down at her, his expression giving her the answer. She began to shake her head immediately, knowing that it wouldn't be a good idea. "I don't think so," she said firmly.

"Midnight, don't fight me on this. If he knows it's his you won't get a moment's peace, and you don't need the hassle right now. Let him think it's mine. He's pissed at me anyway—what else can happen?" But his tone was too light, and Midnight read in his eyes what he thought might happen.

"He'll kill you," she said simply, with no insult intended toward Joe's ability to protect himself.

"He'll try," Joe said honestly. Midnight didn't reply, but her eyes told him that the idea of them fighting that fiercely terrified her. She rested her head on his shoulder, and they lay there like that for the rest of the night, with Midnight sleeping cradled in his arms.

The next day Joe took Midnight to the airport. He held her for a long time at the gate as they waited for her flight to board, his arms around her, her cheek resting against his chest. He whispered to her that she'd better be careful, and to take it easy.

"Take some time off if you have to," he said, feeling her shake her head. He rested his lips against her hair, thinking he should go home with her. He didn't want her facing Rick's fury alone. He pulled away to look down at her; she seemed tired and sad. "Do you want me to come home with you, just till everything calms down?"

Midnight could see the worry in his eyes, and she reached up to touch his cheek. "No, I'll be okay."

Joe wasn't convinced, but he knew how adamant she could be, and he just had to believe that Rick wouldn't resort to actual violence with her.

They heard the boarding call for Midnight's flight. She looked up at him, loath to leave the comfort of his arms. Joe leaned down, kissing her tenderly, his hand cupping her face as he held her close to him. Every woman in the general vicinity watched them with envy, even the married ones. Midnight turned and shouldered her bag, pulling out her gun letter and badge for the boarding attendant.

Once in the passageway, she turned to look back at Joe. He was watching her, and all of a sudden she felt very alone again. Part of her wanted to run back and tell him she'd changed her mind, that she wanted him to come home with her, but her pride and the knowledge that she'd have to be without him at some point gave her the courage to flip him a salute, turn around, and walk down the gangway.

CHAPTER 3

Midnight's flight home was uneventful, as was her drive to her house. She had assumed that Rick had taken Mikeyla with him to Sheila's home, and she knew she had to get her daughter back now. Midnight took long enough to go into the house and drop her bag, then made sure her weapon was secure at her back and grabbed up the extra car seat for Mikeyla before leaving again.

Midnight drove her red classic Corvette up to the Thelands' house. Getting out of the car, she took a deep breath, readying herself to go into the lion's den. She walked up to the front door and rang the bell. The butler opened the door a few moments later. Midnight told him she was looking for Rick Debenshire.

"Is he expecting you?" the butler asked, obviously not surprised that she was looking for someone whose last name wasn't Theland.

"Just get him," Midnight said, not in the mood to play games. She waited outside, eventually sitting down on the steps as she got tired of standing. She heard the door open behind her. She got up, but it wasn't Rick standing there—it was David Theland, looking very dapper in a suit with a brown velvet vest. Midnight figured it was his lounging suit.

"What is it you want, young lady?" he said, as if he had no idea who she was.

"Look, pal," Midnight said, losing her patience immediately. "I don't want to dance with you, so just get my husband the hell out here."

David Theland stared at her as if she were the lowest form of life. "He's not here."

"Like hell he's not." Midnight glanced toward the back of the house, where the garages were. "That's his Mustang back there, unless you've taken up muscle cars, Theland, and you just don't strike me as the type." Her voice was all cop.

"Well, he doesn't want to see you, as I'm sure you can guess." Theland didn't look the least bit chagrinned at having been caught in a lie.

Midnight laughed, an angry, short laugh. "Yeah, well, I really don't care what he wants anymore. So why don't you drag your arrogant ass back into that mausoleum and tell him to get out here, and to bring my daughter!"

Now David Theland had a triumphant look on his face. "Well, I believe that whether she's your daughter or not is a matter of contention right now."

"Look, you obstinate, stupid cow, I'm not going to stand here and argue with you about my daughter's status. I went through labor to have her, and let me guarantee you that that makes her mine." Her expression was angry as she pulled her trump card. "And tell your daughter if she wants Rick's kid so bad, she's just going to have to get herself impregnated, but make sure you remind her that the little stick has to be blue this time before she tries to get him to propose to her!"

Rick threw open the door, having obviously been listening. His eyes burned with anger that Joe had told her about Sheila, and he felt just a bit more of his pride slip away as David turned to look at him. Theland had not been aware of her daughter's conniving the last time Rick and she were together.

"I'll take care of it," Rick said to him, not meeting the other man's eyes. David walked into the house again, closing the door behind him. Rick's eyes narrowed at Midnight. "What the fuck do you want?" he said, holding himself back from moving toward her. She stood two steps below him, about eight feet away. She was looking up at him, her eyes narrowed as well.

"Just get Keyla out here now, Rick." Her voice was strong and clear.

"I don't think so," he said, not affected by her tone.

Midnight stared at him for a long moment, seeing his anger and knowing this was just the beginning of his revenge for what she and Joe had done. She walked up the steps, right up to him, and even though she had to look up at him, she didn't seem the least bit inferior. "Get her, now," she said, her voice low and deadly.

"No," Rick replied simply, and was very surprised when, with a yell, Midnight launched herself into him, shoving him backward against the door he'd come through minutes before. He slammed into it. Midnight had two handfuls of his shirt, her face a mere inch from his. "If you don't go in there and get her now, I will." This time it was a threat, and Rick didn't doubt her for a second.

"They won't let you in," he countered, his voice belying his disgust with her behavior.

"No?" Midnight said, as if honestly surprised. She released him and stepped back. She reached around and grabbed her Beretta from its holster, pulling back the slide ominously. "We'll see about that."

"You wouldn't dare," Rick said confidently.

"Wanna bet your girlfriend's life on it?" Midnight stepped toward him and the door. Rick reached out with lightning speed and grabbed her wrist, yanking her around so that her back was to him. Still holding her wrist, the gun pointed toward the sky, he had his arm up around her neck in a sleeper hold, and Midnight knew if she struggled he'd increase the pressure until she passed out, so she relaxed. After a few minutes Rick decided she'd thought better of her hasty action and let her go. Midnight took two steps away from him, making sure to be out of arm's reach, then turned, pointing the gun directly at his head.

"Now, get the fuck out of my way, or I swear to God, Rick, I'll blow your fucking head off." Her voice was calm this time, and Rick knew that was a definite sign of danger. He stared into her eyes.

"Do it," he said, surprising her.

"I'm serious, Rick."

"So am I," he said, swallowing hard against the knot in his throat. His eyes showed the strain he'd been under since finding out about Midnight and Joe. "I can't go on like this anyway, so do it." His voice was without any emotion at all, but his eyes spoke volumes.

Midnight stared back at him for a long moment. "I just want my daughter." She sounded tired, but the gun never wavered.

"We all want something," Rick said simply.

"Damn it, Rick," Midnight said, her anger igniting again. "You're not the kind of man to hide behind a little girl—don't do this to her."

Rick's eyes closed at the impact of her words. "Don't do this to me," he said quietly. A moment later he turned, opened the door, and walked inside. Midnight put away her gun, not sure what Rick was doing, but aware that she couldn't shoot him anyway. A few minutes later, Mikeyla came running out the door and launched herself into her mother's arms, totally unaware of what had just occurred between her parents.

"Mommy!" she shouted gleefully.

"Hi, baby," Midnight said, hugging the girl close to her. She looked up and saw Rick standing in the doorway, his eyes very serious and, from what Midnight could see, very sad as well. She was beginning to feel like the bad guy here, and she didn't like that. After a long moment she set Mikeyla down and knelt beside her. "How'd you like to stay with Daddy a few more days?"

"How come?" Mikeyla asked.

"Well, because he hasn't gotten to see you as much as me lately, and I just want you to have a chance to be with him too." Midnight made a point of not looking at Rick. "And maybe Daddy can drop you off on Friday, and then we'll spend the whole weekend together. How does that sound?"

"Yeah!" Mikeyla said, happy at the prospect of a whole weekend with her mother.

"Okay, baby, be a good girl and go back inside now. I've got to talk to Daddy for a minute."

"Okay, Mommy. Love you!" the little girl said as she hugged her mother's leg. Midnight knelt down, kissing her cheek and hugging her again.

Mikeyla went back into the house and Midnight stood, facing Rick. He just looked at her, and she stepped forward. "I'm sure we can come to some sort of agreement on shared custody for the time being," she said. But the words didn't change the look in his eyes.

"How could you, Midnight?" he said, and she knew exactly what he was talking about.

Midnight sighed. She turned and started to walk away, but Rick grabbed her from behind, spinning her around to face him. Midnight felt her head swim with the quick movement, but she clamped down on the nausea.

"Answer me," Rick said, unaware of her unstable condition.

"I can't." Midnight's voice was devoid of anger as she concentrated on fighting the waves of nausea. If she threw up now he'd know instantly about her pregnancy, and she didn't want him to find out any sooner than necessary. "No more than you can explain to me why you're with her." Midnight nodded toward the house.

"Midnight," Rick said, his voice softening. He was very affected by her proximity. She saw the look in his eyes and pulled away from him instantly.

"Don't, Rick," she said sternly.

Rick's face changed suddenly. "Oh, I see," he said, his voice turning hateful. "You can cheat on me, but not Joe, is that it?"

"You don't know what you're talking about," she said defensively.

"Yeah, I think I do. You better enjoy it now, Midnight, because he's not gonna be the same when I get done with him." His voice was icy, and Midnight did not doubt what he had said.

"Yeah? Well, why don't you send Sheila out, and I'll see how much damage I can do to her pretty little face," she said venomously.

"Wouldn't be a fair fight."

"Yeah, I know," Midnight said, her voice dripping with sarcasm. "I'd probably have to fight her daddy too, since he seems to fight everybody's battles for them in this house." With that she spun around and walked down the steps. She turned back, her eyes green points of fire. "And if I were you, I'd seriously reconsider trying anything with Joe."

"Why's that?" Rick asked, leaning casually against the doorjamb.

"Because if you touch him, I'll kill you and her." Midnight walked to her car. She got in and, without looking at him again, drove off.

"Nice girl," Sheila said from behind him, and Rick had to fight the urge to slap her. Sheila was always talking Midnight down, especially with her friends. Rick had long since discovered that Sheila was a heartless bitch, but he had stayed with her to get back at Midnight. There had been times when he had wanted to slap a few of the women Sheila hung out with on a frequent basis. They were cold and mean, but they tried to coat it with a veneer of refinement. Rick found himself ever weary of the double-edged statements and looks. Sheila treated him like the errant suitor, all the while assuring him that she cared about him deeply and that she had just been stung by his rejection of her so many years before. She constantly chided him for his poor judgement at having done so. She touted him to her friends as being totally devoted to her now that he had realized the error of his ways.

Little did Sheila know that more than one of her dearest friends had their eye on Rick. His rakish good looks and obvious rebellious streak attracted socialites as easily as it had attracted the girls when he was in the gang in London. One woman, Anastasia Themopoulos, a Mediterranean socialite whose daddy owned a few islands, was particularly direct about her desire to get him into bed. She had approached him on a number of occasions, once when he was actually in the bedroom that Rick and Sheila shared in the Theland home. Rick had gone there to get away from Sheila and her associates for a while. They had started in on "the little people" again, and Rick could only feel sick at their attitude toward anyone they considered beneath them.

He was lying on the bed with his arm over his eyes when he sensed someone enter the room. He assumed it was Sheila coming to look for him, so he said nothing. When he felt well-manicured nails trail along his forearm, he moved it, looking up at the raven-haired socialite.

"Just where I want you," Anastasia said provocatively, her eyes all but devouring him. He had been wearing white pants and a navy blue cotton shirt, open at the throat. When Rick didn't say anything she reached down and touched his chest, her eyes boring into his. Rick sat up, not wanting to be at a disadvantage with this woman.

"I think you should go back downstairs, Ana," he said, eyeing her warily.

"And I think you should think about what I have to offer you," she replied, her eyes indicating her confidence.

"And what's that?" Rick felt very tired suddenly, not in the mood to play games with this woman.

"Anything you want. I could make you a king," Anastasia replied. Her daddy's money had made her bold over the years.

"I see." Rick looked as if he were considering her offer.

Anastasia moved in, pushing him back against the headboard and straddling his body. She was very athletic, and her always-tanned legs were like steel. Rick just looked at her, as if watching an interesting play. She reached out, unbuttoning his shirt and running her nails down his chest appreciatively.

"You are such a beautiful man," she said, making him grin at the irony that she would say something in a way that a man would normally say it to a woman. She took his grin to mean he was giving in, and moved to kiss him. Her lips were aggressive on his, her tongue darting into his mouth, running along his lips seductively. Rick found it almost impossible not to respond to such a sexually aggressive situation. This was the kind of thing that most men dreamed about, and Rick found himself thinking, I should just do her right here. But his sense of propriety overrode the thought almost as soon as it came to him. He placed his hands on Anastasia's waist and hefted her easily from his lap. He set her on her feet at the side of the bed. Anastasia was shocked at such rejection, and became venomous at once.

"You bastard!" she spat. "You presume to reject me? I can have anyone I want, and you think I need you—bah! You're not such a prize!" The haughtiness in her voice ignited his anger, and he jumped up from the bed, grabbing her by the shoulders and backing her up against the wall. His eyes were blazing fire, and Anastasia was excited by the look in them instantly, but she remained outwardly cool.

"What is this?" she said, feigning mild interest. "You think you can scare me, or excite me like some schoolgirl?" She laughed, a manicured, sophisticated sound. "You're a mere passing interest, not my ultimate obsession."

"That so?" Rick said, feigning hurt, the look on his face not changing as he lowered his mouth to take possession of hers. His lips bruised hers with their pressure as he forced her to submit to him, his hands moving suggestively down her body. Within moments she was breathless, moaning for him to take her. She cried out as his lips and hands left her suddenly, and looked up to see his cold smile, his eyes sparkling with victory. He walked out, leaving her standing in his wake.

Anastasia Themopoulos was shocked by his actions, but his aberrant behavior made him all the more appealing to her. She eventually followed him back downstairs, where he was sitting in a chair in the corner of the room, leisurely watching Sheila and her friends as they talked on about the latest gossip. Anastasia looked at him and found him staring at her in return. His lips twisted in a sardonic smile when he saw how that look affected her.

That hadn't been the only time when one of Sheila's friends had tried to seduce him away from her, but it was the most direct. Rick still found it amusing that Sheila seemed to have no idea. He was not currently amused, however. The thought of Midnight sleeping with Joe again just burned in his mind, and all he wanted to do was kill him and take his wife back.

Sheila watched him as he walked back into the house and shut the door. He stood facing it for a long time, resting his head against it. He felt the fury of the confrontation moments before still surging through him. Mikeyla had run off to tell Sheila's mother that she got to stay longer. It had been the little girl's laughter and voice that had brightened his mood the day before when he got back to Sheila's house. He had been very surprised when Midnight had not returned from Sacramento on Sunday, and he had had little choice but to take her to the Thelands with him that night. He had been astounded when Angela, Sheila's mother, had volunteered to entertain the little girl on Monday so he could go into the office for a few hours. Angela seemed thoroughly enchanted with his daughter.

Angela Theland was very attentive to all the occurrences in her household. Although she liked Rick very much, and always had, she did not approve of Rick leaving his wife and sneaking around with Sheila. Angela was fully aware of her daughter's indiscretion; she also knew that Sheila was a spoiled, pampered brat who needed to be taken in hand, but she had long since given up that fight. Sheila was the apple of her daddy's eye, and David always found ways to forgive her outrageous behavior. Angela had, on the other hand, liked Rick's wife the one time she met her, and had found it endlessly amusing that the woman had seen fit to put David in his place on that occasion. David still sputtered angrily if the confrontation was brought up.

Angela had witnessed the encounter between Rick and Midnight on the steps of her house, and had been taken aback by the violence with which Midnight had treated Rick. But she had realized that the woman was basically fighting for her child. Angela could understand that, being a mother herself. Whatever flaws her daughter had, Angela loved her and would do anything to keep her from actual danger. Now, not keeping her from getting burned by someone like Richard Joshua Debenshire, on the other hand, would serve the girl right.

Later that evening, after Mikeyla was asleep in one of the upstairs bedrooms, Angela approached Rick. He was alone in the library, sitting in one of the oversized antique armchairs with his legs stretched out in front of him and a bottle of whiskey in his grasp. He looked every bit the rebellious youth he had been when he dated her daughter years before.

"Rick," Angela said quietly, sounding very American; most older English women called him by his given name. Angela was not English, and she did not put on any airs of trying to be.

He looked up at her, and she could tell that he'd been drinking for a while. He gestured to the chair across from him, trying futilely to straighten up. He assumed she was just putting up with him so her daughter would be happy, like David was doing, so he felt it necessary to try and hide not only his inebriation but also his remorse over his wife.

"You're fine," Angela said, observing his attempt to straighten his clothes. Then she looked more closely at his face. "But you're not, are you?" Her voice was sympathetic, and Rick was surprised.

He didn't answer for a few moments, then shook his head slowly.

"Your wife?" she asked, although she knew the question was rhetorical.

Rick looked at her sharply, surprised by her insight. He was also surprised that she didn't seem upset about him being so distressed about his wife. He was beginning to realize that Angela Theland was nothing like her husband and daughter.

"I saw your exchange earlier," Angela said by way of explanation. "Your wife is rather passionate, isn't she?" There wasn't a trace of criticism in her voice.

"That's an interesting way to put it," Rick replied, grinning. He nodded. "She's very passionate about certain things—work, Mikeyla, and her partner." He sounded angry again as he added the last.

"I think she's passionate about you as well."

Rick narrowed his eyes at her, as if trying to decide if she was crazy. "I think you don't know what's goin' on right now, or you wouldn't say that." His voice held no accusation, but his eyes flashed at the memory of everything that had happened.

"I think I can surmise much more than you realize, and I don't think that one has anything to do with the other—and if it does, it's only because of your current actions with my daughter." Again her voice held no accusation, nor any maternal protectiveness for her daughter's heart.

Rick shook his head. "You don't understand."

"Don't I? Let me see if I have it right. You cheated on your wife with my daughter, your wife found out, and now she's found solace in the arms of another man; and you're still very much in love with her, so you're very angry about the union. Is that right?"

Rick looked at Angela Theland with new respect. It was obvious that she kept better tabs on the goings on around her than he had originally assumed, even if she wasn't totally correct. "Yeah, but you left out a few small details, like that the guy she's sleepin' with is my best friend," Rick said angrily, thinking about Joe's betrayal.

"And he's her partner—and how long has that been?" Angela asked, trying to get all the information so that she could make a fair assessment of the situation.

"Seven years or so, but what difference does that make?" Rick said, angry that she seemed to be trying to find a way to excuse his best friend's treachery.

"And you've been with her for how long?" Angela looked at him pointedly.

"Over four, but—"

"So she's been close to him for longer, and yet you seem to think she should have just sat by and waited for you to finish your affair. Or would you have rather that she slept with someone you didn't know? Would that have been easier for you?"

"That's not the point," Rick said, sounding annoyed.

"Not for you, it isn't," Angela said. She changed tactics. "You still love her, don't you?"

"Why?" Rick was feeling beaten up for the second time that day.

"Because I think you should make sure that she knows that."

"She won't care," Rick said confidently.

"I think you're wrong." Angela stood, patting him on the arm as she walked toward the door. Rick sat staring at the wall for a long time, not sure what to make of the conversation he had just had with his girlfriend's mother about his wife.

CHAPTER 4

Three days later, Randy was fit to be tied. She was lying on the couch with Dick when she received a phone call from one of the sergeants at the academy.

"We have a problem, Cadet Curtis."

"What is it, sir?" she asked.

"It seems that your request for a unit ride-along was turned down by the unit supervisor," the sergeant said, his voice indicating that he thought something fishy was going on.

"Did she give a reason, sir?" Randy asked, her stomach starting to churn with anger.

"Oh, yes, and it's the reason I'm a bit concerned about." The sergeant paused, giving her a chance to chew on it for a moment. Randy couldn't imagine Midnight being unprofessional enough to blatantly blackball her from a unit ride-along; she certainly didn't imagine that Midnight would have actually told them why.

"What reason was that, sir?" Randy asked, trying to keep her voice calm. Dick was watching her now, anger evident on his face as well.

"Well frankly, cadet, she said that she thought your behavior at the academy, as well as that of Cadet Dickerson, was far too aggressive and adversarial, and that she'd prefer that that type of behavior remain outside of her unit. What have you got to say for yourself, cadet?" The sergeant's voice indicated that he believed what Midnight had told him, and that he was seriously considering whether or not he wanted either her or Sarah at his academy.

"I…" Randy stammered, not sure what to say, her anger full blown now. Fucking bitch! was all her mind kept screaming. "Well…" she began again, fighting valiantly to regain her composure. "I believe that I may have been a little insolent, sir, and I am indeed very sorry for that. I will take it upon myself to go and apologize to her. I hope that I will still be allowed to go on the usual departmental ride-along, sir—I know that it is an important aspect of my training, and I certainly don't want to miss any of it." Randy sounded very sincere, and the sergeant couldn't fault her too severely for a one-time insubordination. He would, however, note it in her file, in case it became a pattern later on.

"That shouldn't be a problem, cadet, but just watch your step from now on. You can learn a lot from your superiors, you know, and you should try to be more open to that."

"Oh I will, sir, believe me." Randy's eyes were narrowed as she mouthed the appropriate words. Oh yes, she would learn from Midnight's example, alright.

A half hour later, Randy and Dick sat in front of Midnight's house.

"I'm going in with you," Dick said as she moved to get out of the car.

"It's okay," Randy said. She wanted to do this for herself.

"I won't say a word, I'll just stand there quietly." He held up his right hand. "I swear."

Randy laughed. "Okay, but I want to handle this."

"Yes, ma'am!" Dick saluted her.

Randy walked up to the door and rang the bell.

A few minutes later, Midnight answered, looking tired. Her eyes narrowed when she saw that it was Randy. "What do you want?" she asked, her voice turning to ice.

Randy stepped inside the door, causing Midnight to take a step back. "I want to know why you tried to get me kicked out of the academy." She was instantly angry.

"Oh," Midnight said, pretending to be sympathetic. "Problems, dear? Maybe that'll teach you who to play with." Her look of disgust flicked behind Randy to Dick. "And who to stay away from."

"You bitch!" Randy said, her hand balling into a fist. Midnight saw it and looked at her pointedly.

"I don't think you want to try that."

"Oh, I don't think you know what I want to do," Randy said, surprising Midnight by taking a swing at her. Midnight dodged, but caught her boot heel on the threshold into the living room and fell backward. Randy let her anger drive her after Midnight, trying to take advantage of her downed opponent, but Midnight sprang to her feet. Her eyes reflected the anger that was flooding her veins.

"You dumb fucking kid, didn't you learn anything last time?" She moved deftly as Randy charged her, ending up standing behind the girl. She had mistakenly turned her back on Dick Dickerson though, and he grabbed her, pinning her arms behind her. Midnight didn't fight his hold. Instead, she remained calm until he stepped down the single stair into the living room, then she jammed her booted foot down on top of his. He cried out in pain and released her. She wheeled on him, jamming her shoulder into his chest and shoving him back into the entryway, but he surprised her by grabbing ahold of her as he fell.

Midnight struggled to get up and away from him, but Dick was fast, used to dealing with hookers trying to make a break for it. He grabbed her leg and yanked it out from under her. She fell heavily to the floor, but she launched a kick at his face with her other foot, catching him in the cheek.

"You fucking bitch!" he snarled, grabbing her foot and dragging her over to him. Midnight braced her other foot against his chest, pushing herself away and rolling to stand. But Dickerson jumped up right behind her and again grabbed her from behind. When she struggled and kicked him in the shins, he howled. Utilizing his powerful build, he threw the much smaller police officer against the wall. Midnight sank to the floor, unconscious. Randy had watched the entire scene, horrified. She'd never seen Dick so violent, and she was terrified that she had instigated the fight in the first place.

"My God!" she said, staring at Midnight's motionless form, then at Dick, who was breathing heavily. He had a nasty bruise starting on his cheek already. He didn't look the least bit upset; in fact, Randy reflected, he looked proud of himself. He walked over to the leader of FORS and bent down, feeling for a pulse. Randy felt like she was going to throw up, the idea that Midnight could be dead far too much for her to take.

Dick looked up and saw how pale she was. "She's alive," he said, his voice unemotional. "But we'd better get out of here—wouldn't look good, you know." He grabbed Randy by the hand and dragged her out as she looked back at Midnight.

"Shouldn't we make sure she's okay?" Randy knew she was letting things carry her away.

"She's fine, she'll probably just have a bad headache later. No biggy, serves the bitch right for trying to end your career before it even starts. Probably doesn't want you around Joe so she can keep fucking him." He had said the right words, and Randy walked away with him. They got into the car and drove off.

It was almost forty-five minutes later when Midnight woke up. She noted the blood first; her head was bleeding from her contact with the wall. Her body ached everywhere. When she stood up, she grew very dizzy and had to run to get to the bathroom before throwing up. Afterwards, her stomach ached from the violent retching. She looked in the mirror, noting that she looked pretty bad. She had a dark bruise that had started on her cheek, reaching up to her eye. Her head pounded mercilessly.

She looked at her watch and realized that she had about six hours till Rick dropped Mikeyla off. She had taken the afternoon off to try and straighten up and get prepared for a weekend with her daughter. She'd only been home a few minutes when Randy and the wrecking ball had shown up. Reaching into the medicine cabinet, she grabbed a bottle of aspirin. It was the kind that made you sleep; she was hoping that if she could rest a little bit she'd feel better. She took the aspirin and proceeded to throw them right back up. By the time she was done retching, her whole body ached again and her head felt like it was going to come off. She took some more pills, managing to keep from gagging this time. She went into her room and lay down on the bed, kicking off her boots to try and get more comfortable. Within minutes she was asleep.

Rick stopped the car near the door, noting that Midnight's Corvette was parked further up the driveway. He got out of the car, helped Mikeyla out of her seat, and then walked her to the door. He unlocked it and opened it for her. "You go on in, baby." He didn't want to get into another fight with Midnight at the moment. He kissed the top of his daughter's head.

"Bye, Daddy!" Mikeyla said as she ran inside.

Right as he drove up to the Theland house, Rick's cellular phone rang. He picked it up as he got out of the car and walked up the steps.

"Hello?" He closed the front door behind him.

"Daddy!" It was Mikeyla, and Rick could tell she was crying. What did you say this time, Midnight?

"What is it, baby? What's wrong?" Rick said, leaning against the bannister. Angela appeared, surprised at seeing him on his cellular phone.

"Daddy! Daddy!" Mikeyla was screaming, and Rick could feel the hair on the back of his neck stand up.

"Mikeyla!" Rick yelled, trying to get her to talk to him. "Tell me what's wrong, baby. I can't do anything if I don't know. Is it Mommy?" he asked, thinking that Midnight had gotten mad at the child and yelled at her.

"She won't wake up, Daddy. She won't wake up!"

Rick's blood ran cold. "What do you mean, baby? She's asleep?"

"Yes, and there's all this red stuff everywhere."

Rick's knees buckled and he almost dropped the phone. Angela rushed to him, helping him to the stairs. Seeing that all the blood had left his face, she knew something awful was happening. She took the phone from him and put it up to her ear.

"Mikeyla, sweetie," Angela said soothingly. "Honey, I need you to calm down for me. What's happening?"

Mikeyla sniffled, still crying. "My mommy won't wake up. She's asleep and there's all this red stuff." Angela closed her eyes; she knew what had made Rick weak in the knees.

"Okay, honey," she said, not letting any of her panic show in her voice. "I want you to hang up the phone and then dial 911. Do you remember what those numbers look like?" she asked, hoping Mikeyla would listen to her.

"Yes," Mikeyla said, brightening a little.

"Okay, do that now, honey, and tell them what you told me. Your daddy and I will be there in just a few minutes. You've got to be brave for your mommy, okay?"

"Okay," Mikeyla said, obviously buoyed by the idea that she could help. "Will she be okay?" she asked, needing reassurance.

"Sure she will, honey, she's just sick," Angela assured her, not sure if Midnight was even alive. "Now you call, honey." She heard Mikeyla hang up the phone, and then did the same.

She called out for the butler and ordered him to have the car brought around immediately. "Is there a problem, ma'am?" the butler asked, seeing Rick's face.

"Yes, now go—and hurry!"

She turned to Rick, who looked deathly pale. There were tears in his eyes. "Now you," she said, pointing at him, "try to pull yourself together. Your daughter can't see you like this, or she'll panic too." Rick nodded, still feeling quite sick.

A few minutes later, when they were in the car, Angela dialed Midnight's number; the line was busy. She hoped Mikeyla was on the phone with the emergency operator. When they got to the house there was no ambulance, but that wasn't surprising considering it had only taken them ten minutes; Angela had instructed the driver to break every law he had to in order to get them there quickly.

Rick jumped out of the car before it even came to a complete stop. He hit the front door at a dead run and continued his headlong course toward the bedroom. He skidded to a stop in the doorway. Midnight lay on the bed, a dark bruise on the side of her face. He moved closer, and that was when he saw the blood. Mikeyla was right—it was all over the bed.

"No!" Rick fell to his knees. "Midnight! Oh God, please!" He was crying and yelling at the same time.

Angela had located Mikeyla in the kitchen, still talking to the 911 operator; she took the phone from the girl and began answering what questions she could. The operator indicated that an ambulance should be there at any moment. Angela told Mikeyla to go out and tell the chauffer to help flag the ambulance down. Mikeyla was happy to help—she could hear her father's voice calling her mother's name over and over, but she was afraid to go back into the bedroom. When Angela heard the sirens she told the operator that the ambulance had arrived. The operator indicated it was okay to hang up, telling Angela that her granddaughter had been very brave. Angela didn't bother to tell the woman that she wasn't Mikeyla's grandmother, but she thanked her all the same. She walked toward the bedroom. She could hear Rick's cries and knew that she was probably about to see something she really didn't want to. She walked into the room and almost fainted at the sight she beheld.

"Oh lord," was all she said. The young woman who had seemed so powerful only days before looked very small and very frail, lying on the bed in what looked like a huge pool of blood.

"Come on, baby," Rick was saying, tears streaming down his face. Midnight had not moved or made a sound. He had felt for a pulse and hadn't been able to find one. His hands were shaking so badly he prayed that he had just missed it. She felt very cold, and there was no color in her face or her hands.

When the paramedics came into the room they instructed Rick to move away from her so they could work. Rick stood staring down at the woman he loved, not even sure she was still alive. Angela put a supportive hand on his arm. Mikeyla ran into the room, her eyes darting from Rick to her mother. She ran to her father, and he picked her up. She buried her face against his shoulder, her copper-blond hair mingling with his light brown curls, which fell past his shoulders. Rick held his daughter close, praying that he wasn't watching her mother slip away from them. He couldn't control the tears that continued to flow, which made it more poignant when Mikeyla reached up and touched her finger to his wet cheek. She was dealing with this the only way she could, by distracting herself with things like the feel of her father's cheek when he cried. She knew something very bad was happening, and she knew that it had to do with her mother, but she had no idea that the paramedics weren't the magic cure for whatever ailed Midnight. She figured that because they had come, everything would be fine and her mother would sit up in a few moments and hold her too.

Her mother didn't sit up. She lay motionless on the bed as the paramedics worked on her. They had detected the merest pulse and had looked at each other, almost sure that this one wasn't going to make it. It looked like a good portion of the woman's blood was soaked into the bed she lay on. Her blood pressure was alarmingly low. They could see that they needed to get her out of there and into the ambulance; the pressure of the family, including the beautiful child who had hailed them excitedly minutes before, watching them, waiting for them to tell them that she'd be okay, was too much. They didn't want to be there when her pulse stopped all together; they didn't want to hear the child's cries when she realized the woman that was very obviously her mother wasn't coming back, or hear the devastated screams of the man that was obviously the child's father when he lost what was apparently someone he cared for very deeply.

"Okay," Jim Olson said. "Let's move her." They exchanged a look, each knowing what the other was thinking.

"Okay," Tamara Keating replied, her face grave. She hadn't lost a patient yet, and she was beginning to understand what Jim had been trying to tell her in the last year that they'd been partners. She had tried to tell him that he just needed to toughen up, but he had always shaken his head, telling her that she'd understand when it happened to her. Now she was beginning to. She thought about her daughter and husband, and the idea of her daughter growing up without her made her want to cry.

The paramedics moved Midnight to the ambulance. Rick had decided it would be better for Mikeyla if he stayed with her, and they followed in the Thelands' car. Mikeyla's hold on his neck had tightened uncomfortably when the paramedics took Midnight out. Rick was dying inside. He knew that if they didn't tell him anything, they didn't think she was going to make it—paramedics were trained not to give false hope to the family.

The ride to the hospital was excruciatingly long. Rick kept praying that it was a nightmare and he'd wake up soon. Standing at the counter inside, it hit him again that Midnight might well be dead. That he'd never get to hold her again, never have the chance to tell her how much he loved her. He had to hold on to the counter to keep from crumbling. Angela saw the state he was in and made a point of taking Mikeyla off to show her the pretty pictures nearby.

Rick waited for what seemed like forever. Finally, he went up to the front desk and told them that if they didn't find out where his wife was, he was going to go looking for her himself. The nurse could tell by the look on his face that he meant it. "I'll get on it right now, sir," she said, moving his paperwork to the top of her stack. She made some phone calls and found out that Midnight Chevalier was in a critical condition. She had lost an extreme amount of blood, and they had actually lost her pulse a number of times. The nurse did not want to be the one to tell Rick. She called a doctor over and told him what was happening, aware that both the woman in emergency and the man waiting to hear were local police officers. The doctor nodded, understanding why the nurse was unwilling to be the one to give the man the news.

The doctor, Tom Duhane, walked over to where Rick stood staring unseeing out the window. Dr. Duhane saw an older woman sitting not too far away engaged in a conversation with a child of about two years old. The nurse had indicated that the child was theirs.

"Mr. Debenshire."

Rick turned. "Yes," he said, almost afraid to hear what the older man would say. The doctor's expression was grave, and Rick could almost hear him saying, "We did everything we can, I'm sorry." What Duhane did say wasn't much more promising.

"Your wife is still alive, Mr. Debenshire, but I have to tell you that she is in a very grave condition, and it is quite possible that she won't make it through the night. I suggest that you notify any relatives that she may have, just in case."

Rick stared at the man, not sure what he was supposed to say. He felt like someone had just jabbed him in the stomach with a very large bat. Rick found it necessary to sit down, because suddenly the room seemed to be growing darker. Angela moved to him.

"Rick?" she asked worriedly. She hadn't heard what the doctor had said, but Rick's reaction had made her fear the worst. She looked up at the doctor. "She's not—" she began to say, but the doctor shook his head.

"No, Ms..."

"Theland—please call me Angela."

"Angela, she is in a very critical condition, and I'm afraid her chances aren't very good. I was telling her husband that he should notify any relatives she may have." The doctor realized Rick was probably too devastated to do anything, but he hoped Angela might just help out. Dr. Duhane didn't want this young woman dying without her family around her. He told them he would personally go and check on her status, then walked away.

"Rick," Angela said softly, "is there anyone I should call?"

Rick was just staring into space. His eyes had gone dead; his mind was spinning from what the doctor had told him. Midnight couldn't die. She was his life, his love, everything he had. And if she did die, his last words to her had been harsh, angry words. Rick felt the irony weigh heavily on him. The only woman he had ever truly loved, and she could die not knowing that he still loved her.

"Rick!" Angela said, trying to snap him out of his reverie. "Tell me who to call."

Rick looked at her for a long moment, wondering how she was going to explain who she was, but he figured she could handle that part. "Call FORS," he said, his voice hoarse and broken. "Talk to, um, Spider... and I guess her parents, Jack and Carrie Chevalier, they should be listed. Oh my God." Realizing that he was giving a list of people to be notified that Midnight was dying, he couldn't continue. Angela assumed she should contact Rick's family as well, and she wondered if she should try to contact Joe Sinclair. After all, he was Midnight's partner; even if he and Rick were at odds, it would be a moot point if Midnight died.

"Okay," Angela said, talking to him as if to a young child, "now I'm going to take Mikeyla out of here—she shouldn't see her mother in this condition—and..." But she trailed off as she started to talk about what she would do if Midnight died; no point in making it harder on Rick than it had to be. "I'll make the necessary calls, and then I'll be back. Will you be okay?" she asked, knowing that the question was ridiculous.

Rick just looked at her blankly. Angela was almost sure he was going into shock. She made a point of telling the nurse what she thought on the way out. The nurse, already feeling extremely sorry for the man, said she'd keep an eye on him.

Mikeyla asked Angela questions on the way home.

"Is my mommy okay?"

"Yes, dear, the doctors are taking good care of her."

"Like Mommy took care of me when I was sick?"

"Yes, just like that."

"Good," Mikeyla said, seeming satisfied that her mother was being well cared for.

Angela looked at the beautiful little girl she'd grown very fond of in only a matter of days. It almost broke her heart to know that in a few hours her mother might be gone forever. Angela made an extreme effort to hide her tears, not wanting to upset the child any further. When she got home, Angela asked where her daughter was.

"In the dining room, ma'am. Is everything all right?" he asked, concerned about Rick and Mrs. Theland. He liked working for Angela; she was very kind, and never treated him like a servant, unlike her husband and daughter. Rick Debenshire had been very nice as well, although he knew that Rick was going through a rough time right now. Butlers heard a lot more than most people realized.

"No, Fitz, everything's not," Angela replied, her eyes showing her sadness. She knelt down next to Mikeyla. "Mikeyla, why don't you go with Fitz to the kitchen, and he'll get you some dinner and some ice cream too." She looked up at the butler, who was nodding and smiling.

"Okay," Mikeyla said, unaware that she was being bribed.

Angela walked into the dining room. Sheila and David were at the dining room table, eating dinner. They both looked up.

"Where have you been, dear?" David said, his accent very polished. "I've been worried."

Angela looked from him to Sheila and then back at him. "Rick's wife is in the hospital," she said, noting the quick flicker of joy on Sheila's face and feeling disgusted by her daughter's lack of compassion. She pinned the young woman with a look. "She may die, and while I'm sure that might make you happy, Sheila, just remember that that will leave that poor child without a mother. A job to which you are not suited."

"Really?" David said, looking a little contrite himself.

"Yes." Angela looked back at her daughter, who seemed sufficiently cowed now. "I need Rick's phone book—I need to get ahold of some people for him."

"Do you want me to—" Sheila started, but her mother cut her off with a look.

"And how will that go, Sheila?" Angela pretended to hold a phone, and then, in a higher-pitched voice, she mimicked Sheila's accent. "Oh hi, I'm Rick's girlfriend. His wife is dying." She paused. "I don't think so. Just get me the book, dear."

Sheila got up and left the room.

"You shouldn't do that to her," David said when she had gone.

"Do what?" Angela wasn't even close to being in the mood to argue with him over spoiled little Sheila's hurt feelings. "Teach her that having an affair with a married man isn't the best way to go, and that more than just the absentee wife gets hurt in the process? Is that what I shouldn't do, David?" Her voice was sharp, and her husband was taken aback. Angela had always been frank with him, but her sudden loyalty to Rick's wife was surprising.

99

"Why are you crusading for Rick's wife all of a sudden? It seems to me that she's quite capable of doing fine on her own—she's already bagged Joe Sinclair, from what I understand."

Angela wanted to hit him. She looked her husband square in the eye. "You are a heartless and abhorrent old man, do you know that?" That shocked him into silence, and Angela walked out of the dining room. She met Sheila coming down the stairs with Rick's small phone book in her hand. She gave it to her mother, avoiding her eyes. Good! Angela thought. Maybe she's actually learning.

Angela continued up the stairs and into her dressing room. Sitting down on the settee, she picked up the phone on the side table.

Her first call was to Midnight's parents. Carrie Chevalier answered. "Hello?"

"Mrs. Chevalier?"

"Yes, this is she," Carrie said, not recognizing the voice on the other end of the line.

"My name is Angela. I'm a friend of Rick's."

"Rick Debenshire?"

"Yes, Midnight's husband," Angela supplied, wondering what was wrong with the woman.

"Yes, I know." Carrie sounded offended.

"He asked me to contact you." Angela paused, unsure of the right words to say in a situation like this. She tried to think how she'd want to be told if her daughter was lying in a hospital bed, probably dying. She was at a loss. "I'm sorry, Mrs. Chevalier, but your daughter has had an accident." She expected to hear a gasp, a cry, something along those lines—she heard nothing.

Carrie Chevalier waited. She'd received phone calls like this before, some nurse wanting to notify her that her daughter had been shot, or stabbed or something. Midnight was always getting hurt, and she always came through just fine.

"Mrs. Chevalier?" Angela said, wondering what was happening on the other end of the line.

"Yes," Carrie answered impatiently. "Go on. She's been in an accident, and what—she'll be out in a day or two. Did she get into another fight with some gang member, or did she drive that damn Corvette of hers into something this time?" Carrie's voice was strident; she didn't like to be reminded that she knew little or nothing about her daughter's life or what she did with it. She remembered Rick, of course. He had been so kind, bringing their little granddaughter over to see them.

"No," Angela said, thinking that Carrie Chevalier was a heartless woman. "I don't think you understand. Your daughter may be dying, Mrs. Chevalier."

Carrie was quiet for a moment, trying to decide whether she should take this call seriously or not. Finally, she decided that she had better. "Where is she?"

"She's at Mission Hospital. You should get there right away."

"I will, thank you." Carrie hung up.

The next phone call was to FORS. Angela wondered if anyone would be there that late, and she was surprised when a young man answered. "Yeah?"

"Hello," Angela said. "I need to speak with Spider?" The name sounded strange coming from her mouth.

"You got him." Spider wondered who this woman was and why she was calling so late.

"Spider," Angela said, aware that she needed to get this over with. "My name's Angela. I'm a friend of Rick's—he asked me to contact you."

"Okay," Spider said when she didn't continue.

"I'm sorry," Angela said, once again not sure how to put it, "but Rick's wife is in the hospital."

"What!" Spider shot out of his chair. "What happened, how is she, is she okay?" His words tumbled out on top of themselves.

"I'm afraid not," Angela said. "The doctors don't think her chances are very good. I'm very sorry."

Spider was silent as he stood alone in the office that Midnight ran. He looked around, not seeing anything, the tears in his eyes blurring his vision. "Where is she?"

"Mission Hospital. You will let the other members of your unit know, won't you?" Angela wasn't sure how else she'd tell them all.

"Yeah," Spider said absently. "Can we see her?" Angela realized how close Midnight must be with her unit. Closer than to her own mother, it would appear. Angela felt even sorrier for the young woman in the hospital, and was determined to find out more about her.

"I'm not honestly sure," Angela said, not wanting to give him false hopes, but not willing to dash them either.

"Thanks." Spider sounded every bit a young gentleman. Angela had no idea she was talking to the ex-leader of a fierce Laotian gang.

She called the Debenshires next. Rick's mother answered the phone, sounding tired. Angela realized it was very early in England. "Anabelle?" she said, remembering the warm woman she had known so many years ago.

"Yes?" Anabelle said. She wasn't fully awake and didn't recognize the voice.

"It's Angela Theland. I'm sorry to wake you, but Rick asked me to call you,"

"What's wrong?" Anabelle asked, suddenly very awake.

"It's Midnight—she's had an accident. She's in the hospital."

"Oh my lord."

Angela could hear Anabelle cover the receiver with her hand and say, "Robert, wake up, something's happened." Then, into the phone again, "I'm sorry, Angela. Is she going to be okay?"

"I'm afraid the doctors don't think so."

Anabelle gasped. "Oh my lord," she repeated. Angela could almost see her crossing herself. "Well, how's Richard—was he in the accident? You said he asked you to call—is he okay?" Anabelle sounded so concerned, and Angela was relieved to at least be able to tell her that Rick was just fine.

"It's his heart I'm worried about," she said. "He's not taking it well at all, and poor little Mikeyla, she found her mother."

"Found her? Where?"

"Well…" Angela hesitated, not sure how much to say since she really didn't know what had happened or how much the Debenshires knew about Rick's infidelity. "Rick had dropped her off, and she called him minutes later on his cell phone, telling him that Midnight

103

wouldn't wake up. I'm not sure what happened, Anabelle, but it looks very bad. I'm sorry to have to call you with such awful news."

"Well, thank you for taking the time, Angela." They hung up a few minutes later.

****

Anabelle turned to her husband, who was fully awake now. "That was Angela Theland," she said. "Wasn't it Sheila Theland that Deborah said Rick was staying out all hours of the night with?"

"Yes, dear, I believe it was," Robert said, his brows furrowing. "What's happened?"

"Midnight's been in an accident," Anabelle said gravely. "Angela said the doctors don't hold out much hope of her making it."

"Really?" Robert's voice belied his disbelief. He couldn't picture the vibrant, beautiful woman his only son had married dying.

"Robert, we have to go to him. Angela said Rick is devastated."

"Yeah," Robert said, his eyes sad. "I can imagine he is. You're right, of course. We'll book the first flight out this morning."

Anabelle spent the rest of the wee hours calling Rick's sisters. Deborah was stunned, Allison cried a lot. Katherine was predictably unmoved, though Anabelle sensed that her oldest daughter had come to accept Midnight more over the last three and a half years. Katherine had seemed to disapprove of her brother's dalliance with Sheila Theland, and she explained that she thought that if he had been fool enough to get married he should at least honor his vows. Anabelle wondered at the fact that Angela Theland had been the one to call.

A few hours later, she and Robert were on a plane to California. Anabelle hoped she would arrive to good news.

****

Rick sat staring off into space for a full hour after Angela left, feeling like his life was moving in slow motion. Dr. Duhane walked up to him, and Rick couldn't even find the strength to stand and talk to the man. He was just sure this would be the moment the doctor told him Midnight was dead.

"Mr. Debenshire," Dr. Duhane said, kneeling down. "Your wife has had some severe trauma to her head. Do you know what could have caused that?"

Rick looked at him for a full minute, wondering if the man thought he had done it. Finally he shook his head. "My wife and I are separated right now. I wasn't there. She…" Rick's eyes filled with tears at the thought that once again he hadn't been there for her when she needed him. "My daughter found her. She was in bed, like she'd been asleep." He shook his head, remembering the nightmare scene at the house. He knew he'd never forget the sight of Midnight lying in her own blood, her face so pale and lifeless.

"Okay," Dr. Duhane said, looking down at his watch. "She's in surgery right now. We're not sure what's causing the bleeding—she seems to be hemorrhaging badly. We're trying to get ahold of her doctor, to find out if there's any help he can give us." He looked at Rick again. "Mr. Debenshire, do you know anything? Has she had any accidents lately that may have caused some internal bleeding, maybe something she shrugged off as minor?"

Rick was silent for a minute, his mind going to Sacramento, to Joe. Joe might know something. "She's been out of town, but I'll try to contact her partner up there and ask." Rick wasn't thinking of Joe and Midnight together; he was thinking that Joe might have the key to saving his wife's life.

Rick was up and out of the chair in moments. He texted Joe's cell, putting "911" and his radio call code on the end of the message, cussing at himself because he couldn't do anything else. In a last-ditch effort, he called information and asked for the number of the Sacramento Police Department. Dialing moments later, Rick started to feel desperation creeping into him. He got the dispatcher and explained to her that he was attempting to get ahold of an officer who was teaching at the police academy. The dispatcher offered him Joe's office and cell numbers.

"I've got those," Rick said, his voice taking on an edge. "Don't you have a home number for him?"

"Yes, sir, but I'm not authorized to release that number."

Rick wanted to scream at the woman that his wife was dying while she was being an impossible pain in the ass, but he knew it would get him nowhere. The dispatchers at SDPD were just as well programmed; you didn't give out an officer's home number, not even to someone who identified themselves as a police officer. Home numbers led too easily to home addresses, and that got police officers killed.

"Fine," Rick said, trying to keep his voice even. "Can you please call him and tell him that his partner is in the hospital and that I need him to call me immediately."

He sounded so serious that the dispatcher didn't argue with him any further, figuring that calling the officer at his home number and giving him a message would be alright. She took down the number Joe needed to call and hung up. She called him immediately, but received an answering machine. She left the message carefully. "Sergeant Sinclair, this is Amy VanDeveer from the Sacramento Police Department. A Richard Debenshire called and left the following message with me for you. Your partner is in the hospital, and it is imperative that you contact him immediately at area code 619, 555-7211. If you have any questions regarding this message, please contact me at 916-555-5776." She hung up, hoping Sergeant Sinclair would get the message soon.

Joe was on the range when the dispatcher called. The academy class was conducting a night shoot. It was eight o'clock when the message was left, and the class didn't finish up until 10:30. By the time he had packed up his stuff and driven Jessica home, it was almost midnight.

He picked up the message, turning cold as he listened. He knew instantly what was wrong—he didn't know what had happened, but he was sure she was miscarrying. He called the hospital immediately and asked for Rick Debenshire. The nurse called out Rick's name, but no one answered. Joe explained that his partner, a San Diego Police lieutenant, was in the hospital and that he needed to know what was happening with her. He gave the woman his badge number so she'd know he really was a cop—if she had the time to check it out, that was. She told him that Ms. Chevalier was in a critical condition and that she'd come in with severe head trauma. She also had severe abdominal bleeding, the cause of which could not be identified.

"She's pregnant," Joe said. The nurse was taken aback. Why did her partner know that and not her husband? She thanked Joe and immediately messaged Dr. Duhane.

Meanwhile, Joe was paging John Davies with a 911. Davies called a few minutes later, sounding tired.

"John, it's Joe Sinclair. Look, I need a real big favor."

"What is it?" Davies came awake immediately at the urgency in Joe's voice.

"I need your fastest plane and your best pilot to take me to San Diego right now."

"What's going on?"

"It's Midnight—she's in the hospital."

"You got it," Davies said. He called Tom Dilinger and explained what they needed.

"You got it, Chief. Tell him to meet me at the airport in half an hour."

"Thanks, Tom," Davies said, once again extremely pleased to be supporting Dilinger's program.

Within half an hour Joe was at the BNE hangar at Mather Field, and Dilinger pulled up right behind him. Joe could see that Dilinger was on the phone; he talked for a few more minutes, making gestures and shaking his head, then smiled. He stepped out of his Chevy Blazer and walked over to Joe.

"Okay," he said, clapping Joe on the shoulder. "I've secured us a faster transport than my Queen Air. Forestry's going to let me use their Merlin—it's twice as fast. I'll have you in San Diego in an hour and a half, and the chief's sending one of our agents to the airport to get you and take you to the hospital."

"Thanks, man," Joe said, eternally grateful for all Midnight's work with this agency, and for their unwavering support of fellow law enforcement officers.

The aircraft they climbed into was very nice, but Joe was too nervous to pay much attention. He tried Rick's cell a couple times, but there was no answer—the phone was sitting on the hall table at the Thelands' house.

True to his word, Dilinger brought the Merlin in for a landing at the far end of Lindberg Field an hour and a half later. Joe thanked the man once again, and Dilinger told him he hoped that Midnight was okay.

Joe all but leapt down the ramp, not even noticing the bracing cold of the night air. To Joe's surprise, Griff himself waited to take him to the hospital. Griff's eyes were bloodshot and his face was very drawn. Joe knew Griff cared a great deal for Midnight and that this must have been hard on him, not knowing the details. Joe filled in what few blanks he could on the way to the hospital. When they arrived, Griff threw his car into park and they both leapt out, leaving the vehicle at the hospital entryway. Griff hit the arm button for his alarm as he and Joe all but ran into the hospital.

They asked for information on Midnight Chevalier. It was now two o'clock in the morning. The nurse told them Ms. Chevalier was still in a critical condition, but she was hanging on, and that Dr.

Duhane was speaking to her husband in the room down the hall. Griff held back, letting Joe follow the nurse's directions.

At that moment, the doctor was explaining to Rick what they were trying to do for Midnight. "It's a very delicate operation, but we're hoping to have some experts here from Mercy in an hour or two. We're going to operate as soon as they arrive. Now, Mr. Debenshire, we were told that your wife is pregnant. Why didn't you mention that earlier?"

"Who told you that?" Rick said, furrowing his brow. He assumed they'd been told incorrectly.

"I did," Joe said from the doorway.

Rick stared at his best friend for a full minute, and slowly understanding dawned on him. Much as Midnight and Joe had expected, Rick assumed the baby was Joe's and that was why they hadn't told him about it. Dr. Duhane somehow had the presence of mind to step away from the two men.

"You fucking sonofabitch!" Rick snarled. He lunged for Joe, catching him with his shoulder and knocking him to the ground. Rick jumped on him, his fists flying. Joe managed to block Rick's blows, but the wind had been knocked out of him when he hit the floor. He managed to recover enough to land a punch to Rick's midsection, right before security and Griff hauled them apart.

Rick fought against the arms that held him, his face contorted in rage. "You stupid bastard!" he yelled. "You knew she couldn't have any more kids. You knew it could kill her!"

"Yeah?" Joe said, just as venomously. "Then you shouldn't have gotten her pregnant, you fucking asshole!"

All the fight went out of Rick then. He knew Joe wouldn't lie about something like this. Suddenly, he realized it was his fault if she died—he'd gotten her pregnant again. It was all too much, and Rick let out what could only be described as a banshee yell. Ripping his arms free from the people holding them, he ran down the corridor, desperate to get out into the night. He needed to get away from the hospital and all the horrible revelations. He ran straight into the group from FORS, who were in the waiting room, hoping for word on their leader. Tiny went to Rick, surprised at his hysteria. Spider helped Tiny hold him, and Kana and Dibbins were trying to calm him down when Joe and Griff caught up.

Joe stood looking at the motley group. Everyone seemed to notice him at once, and they all called out to him while still trying to calm their friend. Rick finally gave up, sitting down and allowing the members of his extended family to try to make him feel better.

Joe and Rick said nothing to each other. Joe took the chair right across from his best friend; the two men exchanged looks but remained silent. Griff stood behind Joe, watching the FORS members and Rick.

Rick was surprised to notice Jack and Carrie in the waiting room. They had come in a couple of hours before and asked about their daughter. They had been told the same as everyone else—she was still in a critical condition. Rick walked over to them and indicated that if they'd like to join the group, they'd be more than welcome—and was very surprised when they opted to do just that. He made introductions, shocking the FORS team. None of them mentioned Midnight's basic indifference to her origins. Jack and Carrie were extremely surprised that Midnight had gathered such a group together, and that these people were very obviously worried about their daughter. Even Tammy, Spider's very pregnant wife, was there, though her husband kept telling her to at least rest on the couch in the waiting room. The hours ticked by as they waited for word on Midnight.

It was six o'clock the next morning before Dr. Duhane came out to the waiting room. He stood looking at all of the people waiting for word on his patient. Some of them were asleep, others were drinking coffee, but two remained vigilant—her husband and the man he had tried to attack earlier that morning.

Rick looked up, seeing the doctor standing there. He stood and strode over to the man, watching him the whole time. Joe stood up as well, but hung back, aware that Rick had the right to find out how she was first.

"Your wife," Dr. Duhane began, "is a very strong woman." His voice was still grave, but Rick began to feel a glimmer of hope. "She came through surgery very well. She's in recovery and you won't be able to see her for quite a while yet. We've managed to stabilize her blood pressure, but there was a lot of internal damage. It's hard to say what will happen, but we'll watch her closely and hope for the best."

Rick wanted to pass out from relief. She wasn't dead. She'd come through the surgery well. Maybe, just maybe... "When can I see her?" he asked. The doctor had said "quite a while," and Rick needed a time, an estimate—something.

"Let's give it about eight hours, and then you can see her." The doctor looked past Rick. "And your friends can see her a little while after that, but you have to understand she's been through a lot, and she'll need her rest."

"Thank you, Doctor," Rick said, the beginnings of a genuine smile on his face as he shook the man's hand.

Rick turned to the group after the doctor left and told them about Midnight's status. A small cheer went up. Rick's eyes fell on Joe, who was watching him. Joe had nodded when Rick gave the news, not making a sound, not smiling. Now, as he watched him, he wasn't sure what to say. He knew he and Rick were far from reconciled; he could foresee a few more bouts like the one they'd had the night before. Joe was, however, very relieved that Midnight was closer to being out of real danger.

CHAPTER 5

Joe decided to go back to his house to change and shower, before returning to the hospital. When he walked up to his front door, he knew something was wrong. The alarm wasn't on, and he knew he hadn't left it that way. Joe reached under his jacket and pulled his gun out of its holster. He tried the door handle and found it unlocked. Opening the door slowly, he looked around it carefully. He entered the house much in the way he would conduct a search warrant or a raid, with his gun in front of him and his movements swift. He heard sounds down the hallway and moved in that direction. He stepped into the doorway of his bedroom and was stunned to see Randy and a man kissing on the bed.

Joe felt like someone had kicked him in the gut. He had to step back away from the door, away from what he was seeing. He stood with his hand on the wall, trying to force himself to breathe again. The knife in his heart burned deep; he felt sick. Moments later, hot anger flooded his veins. The fury still pulsing through him, he stepped back into the doorway. Randy had obviously heard his movements, because she sat up immediately and looked straight at him.

"I'm sorry if I'm interrupting something," Joe said, his voice dripping with sarcasm. "I thought this was my house."

"Well, I guess you were wrong," Dick Dickerson said, making a point of taking an extra few moments to remove himself from Randy, even though he could feel her trying to push him away.

Joe's eyes shifted to him, and if looks could kill, Dickerson would have dropped dead.

"I'm not wrong about you not belonging here," Joe said, his voice pure ice.

"Well, Randy invited me in, so it's hardly like trespassing," Dick said, purposely baiting Joe.

"If you're looking to get yourself killed, you just keep talkin'."

Randy was watching the exchange, extremely nervous.

"Oh, I don't think—" Dick started.

"What're you doing back?" Randy said, not able to stand it anymore. She had been going crazy for the last twenty-four hours, wondering if Midnight was really okay. That morning, before academy started, Dick had talked her into picking up the rest of her stuff from Joe's, saying that she needed to make a complete break. Randy couldn't help feeling like a thief in the house when Joe wasn't there. And now here he was, home.

Joe turned his icy gaze on her, and Randy almost cringed. "Not that I think you'll care, but Midnight's in the hospital."

Randy was sure that her heart stopped at that moment, but Dick managed to take Joe's attention off her.

"Ah, what a shame," he said, his voice dripping with cynicism.

Joe's jaw tightened, his eyes narrowing. "You have two seconds to get out of my house before I kill you."

Dick climbed off the bed and took a step forward, standing taller—though even if he stretched, he would still be a full head shorter than Joe. "What're you gonna do? Shoot me?"

Joe looked down at the gun in his hand as if he'd forgotten it was there. With an air of casual flippancy he tossed it aside. "No," he said with a wintery smile. He almost sounded sorry. "I'd rather tear you apart with my bare hands."

"Just try it," Dickerson said, all bravado and testosterone.

"Don't!" Randy screamed, jumping up and getting between them. She was facing Joe, and her eyes pleaded with him. Joe met her gaze and felt himself weaken instantly. He wanted to take her and shake her thoroughly, ask her what she was doing with a loser like Dickerson. But he knew he couldn't touch her right now. He was already so affected by her eyes as she looked into his; he needed her to get out. Clamping down hard on his heart, he stepped aside, gesturing toward the door.

"Get out," he said, his voice cold and hard. Randy grabbed Dick by the arm, and with strength she'd developed at the academy, she dragged him out. Joe followed them to the door.

"Randy," he said, with no emotion whatsoever.

She turned to look at him, still holding onto Dick's arm.

"Next time you come here, make sure I'm here, and"—his voice dropped ominously—"don't bring him."

Randy nodded. She wanted to get away from him as soon as possible.

A few minutes later, in Dick's truck, she turned to him. "What the hell were you thinking?" she said, exasperated. "Baiting him like that—are you crazy?"

Dick shrugged, unconcerned. "It was so valiant of you to protect him."

Randy stared at him for a few moments, then started to shake her head and laugh.

"What's so funny?" Dick asked, perplexed.

Randy snickered. "I was protecting you from him."

"What's that supposed to mean?"

"It means," Randy said, feeling a need to strike out at him for putting her in this position, "that Joe would have ripped you limb from limb. You forget, I've seen him fight."

Dick stared at her openmouthed for a minute, not believing what she had just said. She'd never been downright mean before. He turned back to his driving, aware that something was changing between them.

Randy stared out the window, feeling like her life was running in fast forward, that she was headed for disaster. Midnight was in the hospital. Joe hadn't said how bad she was, but she just knew that something was about to happen to her. Randy was terrified. She was a part of what had happened, and she didn't understand why Dick was so calm.

Randy had no idea how worked up Dick Dickerson really was. He was basically ready to panic. He knew that what he had done to Midnight was the stupidest thing he had ever done. He knew that his ass was hanging out there, and all Midnight Chevalier had to do was shoot it off. He wasn't sure what to do; he needed to get away and think things out.

Dick dropped Randy off at the academy, telling her he had things to do and that he'd maybe see her tomorrow. Randy just shook her head and walked to the locker room to get ready for the physical training she had that morning. The knot of fear in her stomach just sitting there, Randy knew she had to wait and see what would happen—she just didn't know how long she was going to have to wait.

Not very long, as it turned out. That morning, Sergeant Tim Maddy stood in front the class, looking very grave. "We've had some bad news this morning. One of our lieutenants is in the hospital. Lieutenant Midnight Chevalier is in a severely critical condition at Mission Bay."

"What happened?" one of the cadets asked, and Randy tensed, wondering if this was when the police officers would handcuff her and take her away.

"It's not known what happened at this point, but we'll let you all know when we hear anything."

****

After talking to the doctor that morning, Rick went back to the house, intent on completing the painful task of removing all signs of Midnight's blood. Upon inspection, however, he found blood in the bathroom, and in the hallway, and in the entryway. There were a few marks on the marble entryway floor, as well as on the wall, making Rick believe that Midnight had indeed fought someone. He had already suspected that she had been attacked, considering the severity of her head wound and the damage to her body, as if she'd been slammed up against something. He suspected that something was the wall he was examining.

Anger welled up in him. She had fought someone, and they had done this to her and left her to die. Rick found himself wanting to hit something, or someone. It had long since occurred to him that had he dawdled any more when he brought Mikeyla home, trying to prove to Midnight that he had just as much right to time with their daughter as she did, Midnight may well have died. Instead of clearing up as he'd planned, Rick decided to contact the crime scene investigation team at the department. They came out and began going through the house meticulously. Rick stood by, watching and waiting.

Unfortunately, they were unable to locate any prints on the door except for Midnight's. It became evident that she had let her attacker in. Rick became even more uncomfortable with that thought; it meant that she probably knew the assailant, and that worried him. If that person knew that Midnight could identify them, they may make another try for her. Rick informed the investigators, one of whom he knew pretty well, that he was going back to the hospital. He told them that he'd arm the alarm, and they should just close the door when they left.

His cell went off as he was driving. It was almost noon. He looked at the number and realized it was Joe's. Dialing, he tried to push away the thoughts of Midnight and Joe together. He knew being mad at Joe at this point would be counterproductive. He also found it difficult to talk to the man who had been his best friend since he was five years old.

"'Lo?"

"Joe, it's me. What's up?" Rick asked briskly.

"Your parents called me, said they weren't sure where to call you..." Joe's voice trailed off, and Rick knew he was thinking of the fact that Rick was living at Sheila's house.

"Well, what'd they say?" he asked, refusing to be intimidated by Joe's disapproval.

"They're here."

"Here? In America?" Rick was shocked. His mother did not like to fly, and his father was never able to get away from his work long enough to come to America.

"Yeah, they said Angela Theland called them, and they were sure you must need them, so they came." Joe sounded envious that Rick had parents he could rely on.

"Wow. Are they at the airport?" Rick realized he was going in the exact opposite direction at that moment.

"Yeah, where're you?" Joe asked, this time with no accusation in his voice.

"Actually, I'm on my way back to the hospital."

"I thought you couldn't see her for another few hours." Joe sounded concerned all of a sudden.

"Yeah, well, what I saw at the house convinced me that one of us needs to be around her at all times."

"What'd you see?"

"Joe," Rick said. His distress was clear; Joe could tell something was upsetting him. "This thing didn't just happen—she was attacked. I don't know by who, but it's very obvious it was someone she knows, because there's no sign of forced entry and the only fingerprints around are hers. I found signs of a fight in the entryway, and what the investigation team determined was her blood in the entryway, hall, and bathroom." Rick's voice took on an almost hysterical edge as he listed the areas of the house his injured wife had wandered to and from. "She was hurt, Joe, and then the sons of bitches left her to die." His voice broke on the last word, and Joe knew there were tears in Rick's eyes at that moment. There was a pretty fair-sized lump in his throat as well.

"We'll get 'em, Rick," he said. "You and me, we'll get 'em. But right now we need to make sure she's safe. I'm assuming that's why you're on your way back there now."

"Yeah."

"Okay," Joe said, switching gears as his mind turned. "I'll pick up your parents. You just get back there and watch her."

"Thanks, man," Rick said, swallowing against the lump in his throat.

Joe left his house a little while later; he didn't see the truck parked just down the road. He drove to the airport in the black Jaguar he rarely used. He had bought it a few years before, needing a vehicle that would fit more than one passenger. Randy had driven it when they were first married, and she'd liked it so much Joe had bought her a white one for her birthday that year. Now, sitting in the car, Joe was surprised that it still smelled a little bit like his wife.

He arrived at the airport and headed for the terminal. He parked in front, assuming he'd get a ticket, but he didn't want to keep the Debenshires waiting any longer than necessary. He found Robert and Anabelle sitting inside. Joe strode over to them, looking haggard and worn out.

He hugged Anabelle and shook Robert's hand, then called a porter over to take their luggage—what little they had managed to throw into a couple of suitcases.

Once they were outside and the car was loaded, Joe opened the door for Anabelle and then the front passenger door for Robert. As he reached the driver's side, Joe leaned over and pulled the parking ticket off his windshield.

"Shit," he muttered, stuffing the ticket into his jacket pocket. He got in and turned to Anabelle. "Rick's at the hospital with her. Like I told you on the phone, she's a little better now, but they still aren't sure…" He trailed off as his throat tightened up. This was his partner he was talking about, next to Randy the most important person in his whole world, right up there with Rick. He wondered as he turned back to start the car if he should tell them that he and Rick were at odds, and why. He decided they'd figure it out soon enough—no point in upsetting things further.

"And how are you, Joseph?" Anabelle asked pointedly. He wondered if she knew about Randy, not sure if Rick had told them anything.

"Well," he said, his face serious, "I've been better."

"We heard about Randy, son," Robert said sympathetically. "We're sure things will turn around. The day of the wedding, it was obvious how much in love the two of you were."

Joe knew Robert meant to be supportive, but he couldn't control the cynical laugh that burst out. "Yeah, at least one of us was really in love." Again, Joe felt his throat tighten, the scene in his home that morning making him angry and hurt as it replayed in his head.

Anabelle and Robert looked at each other, not sure what had happened since Randy started at the academy. They were all silent for a while, but Anabelle wanted to ask a question, and she knew she needed to do it before she saw her son.

"Joseph, what's happening between Rick and Midnight?"

Joe glanced at her in the rearview mirror, not sure what to say. "How much do you know?" he asked, needing a place to start from.

"Deborah told us about Rick staying out a few nights when she was in town, and she said it was with Sheila Theland. When we talk to Rick he is very evasive, telling us that he and Midnight are having problems, but that they're not serious. And then Angela Theland is the one to call about Midnight being in the hospital."

Joe considered his options. He'd known the Debenshires a very large portion of his life, and never before had he been in a situation like this. He knew they needed explanations, but he also knew some of those explanations could hurt them. He didn't want them to think Rick and Midnight's problems had started with him and Midnight being together, but he wasn't sure whether denying it would make him appear more guilty. Robert Debenshire was a lawyer, after all— he was used to that.

"Yeah," Joe said, careful to keep his tone level. "He left out a couple of things." He looked at Robert as they stopped at a red light. "I'm sorry, some of this might be rough to hear, and if you don't want to hear it from me, tell me and I'll let Rick do it."

"No, Joseph," Robert said. "I know you'll tell me the truth, and the whole story. My son tends to leave out the information that might upset his mother and me."

"Or that might get his ass written out of the will for good," Joe said harshly. Robert seemed taken aback, and Anabelle raised an eyebrow at her husband. She had told him he should question Rick more, but Robert had told her she was overreacting. Apparently, she'd been right.

"Go on, Joseph," Anabelle said.

"Well, it was his runnin' around with Sheila that got him in the water he's in. He was out with Sheila the night that Midnight had to return from Sacramento unexpectedly. He'd been with Sheila for the entire three days that she was gone."

"Where was Mikeyla?" Anabelle asked, already appalled with her son's behavior.

"She was with the nanny," Joe said, his voice showing his disapproval. "Anyway, Midnight had managed to bang herself up at the range up in Sacramento—she was up there rallying support for FORS—and she had to come home. She was on painkillers, and her friend at BNE had to drive her home, and he told me she'd had what he could only term as a breakdown when they got there." Joe looked at Robert pointedly. "She already knew more or less what Rick was doin'. Anyway, I found Rick with Sheila that night and basically tried to knock some sense into him. After that he didn't come home or to the office for about four or five days. Midnight filed for a divorce. She and Rick got into a couple of fights about that, but a couple of weeks later, she and Rick…" He paused, glancing back at Anabelle apologetically. "Well, let's just say all the fire hadn't gone out of the relationship. But things just ended after that. Midnight couldn't handle his infidelity—she has a real thing about trusting someone, especially men, and once that's been betrayed, you've basically had it."

Joe paused again as they drove into the hospital parking lot. He parked the car and turned to look at Rick's parents. He knew he had to tell them the rest; he didn't want them to feel like he'd been trying to hide his own guilt in all of this.

"I've been up in Sacramento, teaching at one of their academies. Last week Midnight told me that Randy was cheating on me, and I kind of went on a bender. Eventually she came up to try to talk me down, as it were." He took a deep breath, realizing this was probably the hardest thing he'd had to do in a really long time. "Well, Midnight and I ended up, well, together. I don't know if you two know about her and I, and I guess if you don't this would probably seem like a really rotten thing to do, but—"

"Joseph," Anabelle said softly. She was nodding. "We know about your and Midnight's past relationship." There was no anger in her voice, no accusal, and Joe found himself very relieved. It was as if Anabelle and Robert were his own parents, and their outrage would be more than he could take at this point.

"Yeah, well," he said, abashed, "I guess it's not past anymore." He looked at Robert, wanting to know if his best friend's father was irritated about the situation. Robert seemed surprised, but not angry. "Anyway, the thing is, Midnight came back in the middle of the week and was supposed to have Mikeyla for the weekend. I guess when Rick dropped Mikeyla off, Mikeyla found Midnight on her bed, unconscious. She called Rick, and Rick got back to the house—I guess Angela brought him. Anyway, they got Midnight to the hospital, and here we are."

"But what happened to her?" Anabelle asked.

"Well, we're not totally sure. Rick found signs of a struggle at her house, and he thought that she had been thrown against a wall. When they got to her she had managed to move around the house, and ended up in bed somehow, but she had hemorrhaged badly and—" He looked at both of them, aware that he was about to shock them. "She was pregnant."

Anabelle closed her eyes, and Robert shook his head, as if trying to deny what Joe was saying.

"When she and Rick were together some two and a half months ago, she got pregnant. Rick didn't know." Joe found it necessary to tell them the last, not wanting them to think their son was totally cold-hearted.

"But you did?" Robert asked insightfully. Joe just nodded, clearly troubled now.

"Let's go in," Anabelle said after she recovered her composure. She felt it was more important to be with her son right now. Not only might he lose his wife, but he had already lost a child in the last twenty-four hours.

Rick had forced the doctors to let him in to see Midnight when he arrived back at the hospital. He told them it was police business and that her life may be in danger—not just medically. The doctors had no choice. Rick shoved past them and the security guard trying to stop him, the look on Rick's face making the guard realize he wasn't paid nearly enough to be killed trying to keep a cop from seeing his wife.

When Rick entered Midnight's room and saw her lying there, he had to lean against the nearest wall, closing his eyes and hoping he wouldn't pass out. When the shock wore off, he walked over to the bed. For all intents and purposes, Midnight looked like she could be dead. She had no color, and her breathing, although assisted by a machine, seemed too shallow to support life. When he touched her hand it was cold. He had to keep telling himself that as long as the monitor was still finding a heartbeat, she was alive. There were IVs running into her arms, one of which was blood. The doctors had told him that the blood loss alone could have easily killed her. They were attempting to replace the vital fluid as rapidly as possible.

Noting that there were no chairs in the room, since visitors weren't allowed in this section of the hospital, Rick knelt down. He thought about his strict Catholic upbringing, and found it ironic that even though he hadn't been in a church since he and Midnight were married, not only had he been praying a lot in the last eighteen hours, here he was now, kneeling too.

"I wouldn't do this for just anybody, you know," he whispered next to his wife's ear. He longed for her to wake up and tell him she wasn't just anybody, or to slug him for his behavior of late—anything, so long as she woke up.

But she didn't move, and Rick found himself watching her face intently. He had begun to think in the last few hours that this was some kind of wrath from God, a consequence of his adultery, that God was saying, "If you can't be good to her, I'll take her." Rick reflected that it was probably what Joe had been thinking when they fought.

He couldn't think about it. His mind veered violently away from any thought of Midnight and Joe together. It made him feel like he had over four years ago when he met Midnight. He had imagined what it would be like to have Midnight look at him in the way that she looked at Joe. Joe had obviously meant so much to her. They had fought, and come together and fought again, but when the chips were down, it was Joe that Midnight had clung to when a member of FORS had been killed. It was Joe who was able to talk her down and remove her firearm from her grasp. Rick hadn't been able to get through— she had locked him out, literally and psychologically. But when he

127

and Midnight got married, when he found out she was carrying Mikeyla, it had felt so incredible that someone so fantastic could love him and want to have his child. She was radiant the day of their wedding, and looked at him with all the love and trust with which she had looked at Joe—even more. And now, he had screwed all that up. He had betrayed her trust and this was his punishment.

"Come back to me, baby," he whispered, "and I swear I'll make it up to you. I love you." There were tears in his eyes, and he put his head down on the bed next to her, his hand still holding hers. He needed to be close to her, needed to be there, in case she woke up, or... Again his mind shrank from the thought. He couldn't think about what he would do if she actually died. Every nerve in his body protested the idea.

Before Anabelle Debenshire walked into Midnight's room, she took a deep breath. The doctor had told them Midnight was still in a dire condition, and that they might be surprised by her frail appearance. The doctor had no idea what a contrast saying the words "frail" and "Midnight Chevalier" in the same sentence really was. When Anabelle saw her son, his head resting on the bed next to Midnight, his hand holding hers, she instantly felt tears sting her eyes. She realized how difficult it must have been for Rick two years before, when Mikeyla was born. They had almost lost Midnight then as well, and Rick had been frantic. Anabelle had been sorry she hadn't been able to be there for him; she had been glad that Joe was there to support him. But now, things were different.

Anabelle walked over to her son and touched his shoulder gently. Rick started, his head snapping up, his body tensing. When he saw that it was his mother, he started to get to his feet, but his legs wouldn't cooperate. He'd been down on his knees for so long that his legs had basically gone to sleep from the knee down. Joe, who had come in behind Anabelle, reached over and pulled Rick up, steadying him as his mother held him in an embrace.

Rick was crying. Seeing his mother had brought all the anguish and worry out. Joe went to find some chairs for the Debenshires; he also needed an opportunity to get out of the room. The sight of his partner lying there, looking all but dead, had been more than he'd been prepared for. He'd seen Midnight in a lot of bad situations, with a lot of injuries, but he'd never seen her like that. He had felt like someone had just crushed his lungs, and he couldn't breathe.

Standing outside the room, he leaned against the wall, sliding down to sit on the floor. He was breathing deeply, as if he were in actual, physical pain. Until then, he hadn't really faced the possibility that she could actually die. And now the prospect of the hours of waiting just seemed too much to handle. Joe found himself wanting Randy there with him, wanting her to hold him and tell him everything would be okay. He was surprised at that; he had always been the strong one in the relationship. Or so he had thought—it was slowly dawning on him that he had depended on Randy as much as she had depended on him. He stood up and walked over to the pay phones. Without thinking, he dialed Randy's cell phone number. He didn't know if she was still carrying it, or if she'd even be near it at the moment, but he knew he had to try.

Randy was very surprised when her cell phone rang as she and Sarah were having lunch in the cafeteria. She always kept it handy when she could, out of habit; Joe had called her on it many times to tell her he'd be late, or how a bust had gone. Randy hadn't really realized it was

Joe's influence that had given her the habit until she answered and, to her shock, heard his voice.

"Hello?" she said casually.

"Randy," Joe said. He sounded despondent, and Randy almost choked, thinking he was going to tell her Midnight was dead.

"Joe! What's wrong?" she said, forgetting about her own situation and beginning to worry about him—again, out of habit.

"I just…" he said hesitantly. "I need you, please." His voice was so quiet, so desperate, that Randy couldn't even consider telling him no.

"Where are you?" she asked.

"At the hospital. Can you come here?" he said, imploring.

"I'll be there as fast as I can." She hung up.

Sarah was watching her carefully. "You'll be where as fast as you can?" she asked, her tone indicating that she thought Randy was just running at the sound of her master's voice, something she had accused Randy of over and over.

"Sarah! You don't understand, and I don't have time to explain. Please, just tell them I'll make up the time, or whatever. Look," she said, trying to sound more patient now, "I need to borrow your car. Dick dropped me off this morning…" She trailed off as she thought about the morning's confrontation with Joe. As Sarah handed her the keys, still looking uptight, she wondered idly whether Joe would bring that up. But she didn't think about it anymore as she sprinted across the campus and headed for Sarah's beat-up Camaro.

The drive to the hospital was quick, but Randy still found herself pressing the pedal hard. She wanted to run every red light she encountered. She wasn't sure what had prompted Joe to call her, but she wasn't going to let him down. The guilt she felt over what Dick—and indirectly she—had done made her long to make it up to Joe. At the hospital she parked in a handicapped space, not caring about the huge ticket she'd probably get, and rushed inside. When she was directed to Midnight's room, she walked as quickly as she could. She saw Joe in the hallway; he was pacing back and forth, and Randy wondered as she approached him why he wasn't in the room with Midnight.

"Joe," she said tentatively, starting to worry that he'd rethought his phone call to her. But when he turned to look at her, the complete misery on his face made her run the last few steps, straight into his arms.

Joe held her close, his head bent to hers, his hands entwined in her hair. After a long time, she finally felt his hold lighten. She looked up at him, her hand automatically going to his cheek to brush away the tears. Joe's eyes closed in response to her touch.

"How is she?" Randy asked softly.

Joe shook his head. "The same, I guess." He allowed her to guide him to the couch just behind them.

"She's going to be alright though, right?" Randy said, her voice tinged with an anxiety that Joe didn't understand.

"Randy, they don't know. She's still critical and doctors aren't saying anything right now. Which is good, considering they were predicting that she wouldn't make it through the night less than twenty-four hours ago."

"God," Randy breathed, realizing there was no way she could stay with Dick a moment longer, knowing what they'd done.

Inside the room, Rick was sitting in the chair next to Midnight. Anabelle and Robert sat behind their son. Rick had reached over to brush Midnight's hair back when he saw her eyes flicker. "Night," he said. He wanted her to wake up, but knew that could still be hours away.

Midnight moved her head just slightly and let out a low groan. Rick immediately reached over and pushed the button for the nurse, who arrived a minute or two later, right as Midnight opened her eyes. The nurse checked her blood pressure and then the machines she was hooked up to. "Her blood pressure is better," she said to Rick. "I'll go contact the doctor. He should be able to tell you more."

Midnight had been gazing up at the ceiling while the nurse worked on her, but had since closed her eyes, as if watching the woman's quick movements was too much. When the nurse walked out, she opened her eyes again and looked at Rick. Her expression was blank and emotionless. It was as if she was trying to put everything together in her head.

When the door opened, her gaze shifted to it. Joe walked in with Randy trailing behind him. Midnight's eyes went to Randy and narrowed. Joe assumed she was mad at him for obviously being weak and needing his cheating ex-wife. He didn't see the terrified look on Randy's face.

Midnight looked back at Rick, then behind him. Anabelle and Robert were standing now, and seeing them, Midnight gave a half-smile, almost a grimace. She started to move, as if trying to sit up.

"Don't, Midnight. You need to stay down. You've been hurt pretty bad, and you can't get up just yet. Okay?" Rick's voice was firm but soft.

Midnight looked at him, as if wondering who he was to be giving her orders, but she lay back again.

Joe moved to the edge of the bed. He needed to see that she was awake and conscious of what was happening around her. Midnight stared up at him. His face was very solemn, and her eyes welled with tears at the sight.

"Hey," Joe said, his voice deep with emotion and relief. "Knock that shit off." He grinned at her, and she tried to smile too. He saw her right hand, the one without an IV in it, move to her stomach. She looked up at him; he shook his head sadly. She closed her eyes, and he saw a tear slip down her cheek. It tore at him, feeling helpless.

"Night," Rick said, having watched the exchange between his wife and Joe. "What happened?" He was desperate for her to tell him—he was going crazy, imagining things.

Midnight opened her eyes again, the tears still evident in them. She looked at Rick for a moment, and then her stare moved behind Joe to Randy. Randy felt her heart flutter. She was sure Midnight was about to tell them that she and Dick had caused this, and Joe would arrest her, or worse. Midnight's eyes took on a knowing look, but only Randy understood it, and then she looked at Rick again.

"I…" Midnight started, her voice a whisper. "I can't remember." Her glance flicked to Randy again, and she saw the relief evident on her face. It was a good thing that everyone in the room was looking at Midnight, because had they looked at Randy, she was sure they would have known everything.

"Don't worry about it," Joe said. "You've been through a lot—maybe it'll come back later."

Midnight nodded as her eyes closed again. She slept, and Rick's parents basically threatened to drag their son out of the room if he didn't go voluntarily. "You need to eat, Richard," Anabelle said, sounding every bit the overprotective mother. "And some sleep might do wonders." Finally Rick acquiesced. He knew he couldn't fight both parents, and felt a lot better that Midnight had finally regained consciousness. They waited a few minutes for the doctor to arrive, and when he did he told them Midnight was seemingly out of danger. Rick was so relieved he felt like crying again.

"Now," Anabelle said, "will you please let us take you somewhere and get some nourishment in you?"

"Okay, okay," Rick said, holding up his hands.

Anabelle turned to Joe. "Joseph, Randy, will you join us?"

Joe shook his head. "Thanks, but I think I need sleep more than I need food right now."

"Well, that's probably a good thought as well," Anabelle said, smiling. It made Joe feel good to have someone looking after him again. He hugged Rick's mother and shook hands with Robert. He looked at Rick, who was watching him, obviously not sure what he should say or do. Then Rick put his hand out, and after a moment's hesitation, Joe took it.

"Thanks for pickin' up my parents. I'm guessing you'll be checking in at the office and the like." Joe nodded. "I guess I'll see ya later then," Rick said, obviously still uncomfortable with the situation between them.

"Yeah," Joe said somberly. "I'll be back." He walked out of the room with Randy trailing him. She followed him out to the parking lot.

"So," she said, feeling unsure of herself with him. It reminded her of when they had first met, when she'd been his shy secretary. "Where're you going?"

"Home, I guess," Joe said, reaching his car and turning to face her. "What's on your agenda for today?" he asked, his voice overly casual.

"Home, I guess," Randy said, staring up into his eyes.

Joe looked at her for a moment, as if he were searching for something. He went around to the passenger's side and opened the door for her. Randy slowly walked around the car and, looking up at him, got in.

They were quiet on the way to the house. Randy looked over at her husband of over three years. He looked exhausted; she didn't know he hadn't slept in going on thirty-two hours. He hadn't been able to sleep that morning, after the confrontation with Randy and Dickerson. He'd taken a shower, then sat on the couch for a while, staring off into space, not sure what else to do. He knew he should sleep, but had been unable to get the vision of Randy and Dickerson out of his mind. Not long after that, the Debenshires called.

As he drove up to the house, Joe wondered mildly what was going to happen between him and Randy. He had been so upset when he called her, and so relieved when she came to the hospital without arguing. Now here she was, with him. He wanted to talk to her; he wanted to understand what was happening with them. But he didn't have the energy, nor the desire to change the quiet, comfortable mood between them to one of anger and fighting. Not yet, anyway.

As he got out, he noted that she was opening her own door. He wondered if Dick didn't do things like open doors for women. Joe walked up to the house and punched in the code, then opened the door for Randy. His cell went off as he closed it behind them. It was Spider.

"I'll take this in the other room," he said, and walked down the hall to the bedroom.

Randy went into the kitchen thinking she would make something for him to eat. Eating was always a low priority for Joe, especially when there was a crisis. She found that there was practically nothing in the cupboards or the refrigerator. She remembered that Joe had been in Sacramento until the night before. Using her cellular phone, since Joe was on the house phone, she called the local Chinese delivery place that they always used and ordered some of Joe's usual favorites.

To her surprise, they were at the front door fifteen minutes later. She had been sitting at the kitchen table, reading over the newspaper that had been on the front step, not wanting to intrude on Joe. She paid the delivery boy and gave him a fair-sized tip for being so quick.

Going back into the kitchen, she reached into the refrigerator and pulled out the bottle of wine that was just about the only thing in the appliance. She walked over to the china cabinet, trying to ignore the Dresden set that they'd received as a wedding present from one of Joe's many relatives as she reached in to get a wine glass. She looked at the elegant crystal in her hand. It was Waterford, a very beautiful glass, and Randy found herself thinking about the times that she and Joe had sat in this dining room. They'd had many meals at the table. They didn't use the china that much; Joe said it was too uptight for his tastes, and Randy agreed with him. They had always used the crystal though—Joe said it made the wines he introduced her to taste truer.

He had introduced her to so many things. He'd taught her about wine, and elegant foods. She remembered the time she'd told him she was a Pepsi and Fig Newton kind of a girl, not a champagne and caviar kind. To her surprise, that night Joe poured a can of Pepsi into the Waterford champagne flutes and served her Fig Newtons on a crystal tray. She had thought she'd die laughing. Randy had told him she thought Pepsi tasted even better in the crystal, and Joe had laughed uproariously.

Later that evening they'd looked through the photographs that he'd retrieved from his parents' home. She'd been so enchanted with the pictures of him when he was a baby, imagining what their own child would look like. She'd seen the pictures of his parents and had once again realized how different her and Joe's lives had been, and had marveled at the fact that she was married to him.

Now, standing in the dining room, a bottle of wine under one arm, Chinese takeout in one hand and a crystal wine glass in the other, she looked around. Suddenly, everything seemed different. She felt like the woman in the movies who gives up everything she loves for all the wrong reasons. The woman people denigrate for her stupidity, the woman who dies alone and unhappy at the end of the movie. Randy realized at that moment that she had thrown her happiness away with both hands and had embraced something that she thought she wanted. She still wanted to be a police officer, but she also still wanted to be Mrs. Joseph Michael Sinclair. She wondered whether she was being superficial, trying to determine if it was the money and elegant lifestyle she missed or Joe.

She headed toward the bedroom and found Joe still on the phone. It was obvious it was the office, because he was delegating some of the routine work that needed to be kept up while Midnight was out. He looked up at her when she entered, noting her burden. He smiled at her, and Randy felt her breath quicken just a bit. As she had been weeks before, she was surprised by the effect his appearance had on her, and when he smiled at her, she felt a strong tug at her heart.

Randy set the bag on the nightstand, handing Joe the glass and opening the wine. She made a show of smelling the cork and fluttering her eyelashes as if the bouquet were overpowering. Joe watched her every move and grinned at her humor. Randy poured the wine into the glass and replaced the cork. She proceeded to pull out the little boxes of Chinese food, opening each and tilting them toward him so he could see the contents. Joe nodded, as if approving the menu. He motioned to his glass and then pointed to her. Randy reached over, took the glass, and, pretending to misunderstand him, lifted it to her lips and drank. She watched his eyes as she did so. He raised an eyebrow at her and grinned.

"Okay, Spider," he said into the phone, having been half-listening to what the man was saying. "That's going to be the drill for the next few weeks, at least. Yeah, she's doin' a lot better now. Maybe you guys can come see her later tonight." He listened again. "You got it, I'll see you tonight." Spider had suggested that they all meet for dinner, so he could brief everyone on what was happening. Spider knew the members of FORS were reeling from Midnight's brush with death, and they needed the reassurance of their second-in-command's presence.

Joe hung up the phone and looked at Randy. "And what have you been doing?" he asked mildly, his grin back.

"Cooking," Randy said simply, then indicated the takeout boxes. "I just put the food in those for convenience."

Joe nodded. "Really now?"

"Yeah, I guess you didn't know I could cook Chinese, huh?" She shrugged and, with a humorous glint in her eyes, handed him one of the boxes along with the chopsticks that had been in the bag. "I thought you probably needed to eat something." Her voice was quiet; she was worried that maybe her concern for him seemed inappropriate, considering the situation.

Joe noted her change in mood. "You're probably right." He looked at her, his eyes trying to catch hers. "Somethin' tells me I interrupted your lunch this afternoon, so you probably need to eat too." He patted the spot next to him on the bed, and after a moment's hesitation Randy sat down.

Joe ate a few bites and then held up the box, a shrimp between the chopsticks, gesturing for her to take some. Randy leaned forward, and Joe fed it to her. They ate the rest of the food in much the same manner. Occasionally, Joe would drink some wine and offer her the glass. By the end of the meal, they were feeling very companionable. Joe had switched on the television while they ate, trying to keep from having to talk, not wanting the spell to be broken.

Putting the last box on the nightstand, Joe leaned back against the headboard. Throwing caution to the wind, Randy sat between his legs and leaned back against him. Joe's arms came around her, and she felt him relax. They continued to watch whatever was on the television. Joe had reached over to pick up the bottle and refill the glass. They sipped the wine and reveled in being close to each other again. Both of them were afraid to try to move beyond this, though, afraid the other would rebuff the advance.

After a while, it became obvious to Randy that Joe was indeed exhausted. His hands had begun to get a little shaky, and knowing Joe the way she did, that was a sure sign of fatigue. She sat up, turning to look at him. His eyes were indeed very bloodshot, as well as weary. She got up from the bed, shaking her head at him reproachfully. She reached over and pulled off his boots, and went to remove his ever-present shoulder holster. Joe made no move to stop her, just watched her. She laid his holster carefully on the chair next to the bed, knowing that he liked to have it close by at all times. With a mischievous grin, she grabbed ahold of his ankles and yanked on them, pulling him so that he was actually lying down. Then she picked up the remote and turned off the TV. She turned to him, disconcerted by the way he was watching her eyes, but determined to make him go to sleep.

"Now," she said softly, "close those baby blues." When he didn't, she raised an imperious eyebrow, indicating that he was countermanding her order. Joe grinned tiredly, but refused to close his eyes. "Do it, Joseph Michael, or else."

His grin turned mischievous, but his eyes were now half-closed, the wine starting to take its effect on him. "You know I hafta ask," he muttered.

"Yeah," Randy replied, hands on her hips. She sounded a lot like Midnight when he didn't listen to her. "Well don't, because you won't like the answer."

"I doubt that," he said, his voice still very low, but huskier.

"Well, don't," Randy repeated, trying to sound gruff but not succeeding. The tone of his voice was affecting her more than she was willing to admit.

"Will you be here when I wake up?" he asked, his words belying his concern.

"Yes," Randy said, but she could see the doubt in his eyes. She realized that her leaving him had affected him more than she had comprehended. "I will be," she said softly. "I promise."

Joe still didn't look convinced.

Randy sighed. "Okay, what if I stay right in here with you. I'll sit right here in this chair, and I won't move. Will you go to sleep then?"

Joe grinned at her and nodded, looking very much like a child who wants another story read to him before bedtime. Randy couldn't help but smile as she sat down in the chair, and he closed his eyes, the grin still on his face.

It amazed Randy how different Joe was with her. He was this big, tough, gun-carrying cop, and yet when he was with her, he was so sweet and funny, even cute sometimes, like now. Many people wouldn't believe her if she tried to tell them how he was when they were alone together. She'd even tried to convince Dick when they'd talked about Joe. Dick had told her that he didn't understand how she could be so sweet and be with a guy like Sinclair. "That guy hasn't got a sensitive bone in his body!" he'd said when she told him Joe could be very sweet. She had tried to explain it to him, talking about Joe's habit of sitting out on the deck with a glass of wine at sunset. "He doesn't even take his gun out there, that's how serious he is about trying to put a few minutes between himself and the job." Dick had shaken his head, not believing her. He said she just wanted to romanticize Joe to justify her dependence on him. Randy had given up, feeling that it was a moot point anyway. How Joe had been and how he was with her at that time were two different things.

After fifteen minutes, Randy got up and crept out of the room. She went into the kitchen and picked up the newspaper. When she went back into the bedroom, Joe's eyes were open, and he looked at her with a sardonic grin.

"I'm back," Randy said, smiling. "You can go back to sleep now."

"Thank you," he said, still grinning as he closed his eyes again. Randy found it amazing that he had sensed she was out of the room.

She read the newspaper for a while and found herself getting sleepy. She ended up putting down the paper and curling up. She awoke a little while later to feel herself being lifted from the chair. She looked up as she was laid down on the bed. Joe smiled down at her. "You looked uncomfortable," he said, and lay down next to her on his side, his arm resting casually across her stomach. His face was just above her, and she turned her head so that she faced him, her cheek just under his. She could feel his breath tickling her skin. They fell asleep close together.

The sun was setting when Randy stirred. She moved carefully, remembering where she was. She knew how easily Joe was awoken. But it was already too late; when she looked up at him, his light blue eyes were looking back at her.

"How do you do that?" Randy asked, exasperated.

"In the business we're in, it becomes a survival instinct," he said. Randy noted his use of the word "we," and she wondered if he had meant to include her or if he was referring to himself and FORS.

"We?" she asked, wanting to satisfy the curiosity.

"Yeah," Joe said. "Me, Rick, Midnight, and…" He looked at her. "You."

Randy smiled, feeling suddenly wonderful. She could still have him and be a cop. "What made you change your mind?"

Joe shrugged. "I didn't have a choice, did I? I'm not saying that I like it, because I still don't, but someone told me recently that I needed to let you go your own way."

"Who was that?" Randy asked, surprised that he'd listened to anyone about this particular subject.

"A friend, up in Sacramento," Joe said quietly. Something had changed in his eyes all of a sudden, but Randy was anxious to get things back on track. Impulsively, she kissed him. After a few moments, she felt his hand tighten at her waist, and he dragged her closer. Their lips melted together, and once again Randy remembered the feel of him, and her own reactions to that feeling. Suddenly, though, Joe was pulling away, shaking his head.

"Randy, wait," he said, his voice rough with reigned-in desire. "I can't do this, not now."

"What? Why?" Randy felt spurned, and angry about it.

"Look." Joe sat up, leaning against the headboard and looking down at her. "There's something you need to know." He didn't sound apologetic, but she could already tell it was not going to be a nice conversation.

Randy sat up too, unconsciously putting a few extra feet between them. She had become wary, sure she wasn't going to like what he was going to tell her. Maybe it was about his "friend" in Sacramento, she thought.

"Okay," she said, taking a deep breath and blowing it out.

"About a week and a half ago, I called Midnight, and she told me about you and Dick." He looked straight into her eyes, and she felt belatedly guilty. She lowered her eyes. "Anyway," he continued, resting his head back against the headboard and staring up at the ceiling. "I spent the next few days climbing inside a bottle, and pretty much enjoying it." He paused and looked at her again, his eyes accusing, his pain at her betrayal clear.

"Joe," Randy started to say, not sure what she could tell him that would make any difference now, but he was shaking his head at her.

"I'm not looking for an apology now, Randy. Nothing can change what's happened, but you need to know it all."

"Okay, so what is all of it?" Randy asked, once again sounding a lot like his partner.

"Midnight ended up coming up to Sacramento to drag me out of the hole I'd crawled into. She told me then that she was pregnant." When he paused again, Randy started to shake her head, thinking he was telling her the child was his.

"Joe, I don't think I want to hear this. I mean, if you got your partner pregnant, then—"

"Jesus Christ, Randy!" Joe said angrily. "You really do think Midnight and I slept together while you and I were still together."

"Didn't you?" Randy asked, her voice indicating that she thought the question was rhetorical.

Joe looked at her for a long moment, shaking his head slowly. "Would you believe me either way?" he said softly.

"Doubtful," Randy said. Her expression seemed to be closing him out.

"Well, it's a moot point anyway. I don't have to convince you. She and I spent some time together up there and—"

"And you slept together," Randy said triumphantly.

Joe shook his head. "Does that make you happy? Or does it just make you feel less guilty?" His words struck her, momentarily knocking down her bravado.

"So what you're telling me," she said, her face a mask of anger and cynicism, "is you won't sleep with me now because you won't cheat on her?" Randy couldn't believe this was happening. Her husband wouldn't cheat on his girlfriend with her, his wife.

"What I'm saying," Joe said calmly, not rising to the bait, "is that I don't know where she and I stand right now. I don't know that she's not depending on me to be there for her, and I can guarantee you I will be."

"Yes, you always are, aren't you?"

"And you knew about Midnight and me when you and I got together," Joe retorted, his voice turning to ice.

"Yes, but I guess I didn't realize she would come before me."

"No one ever came before you, Randy," he said very seriously.

"Well, she certainly came right after me now, didn't she?" Randy said, emphasizing the word crudely.

"Yeah," Joe said, nodding. "You could say that. She was there for me—and just where were you at that point?" He raised an eyebrow at her.

"Oh, so I slept with someone and you had to do the same. What, does that make us even? Does it make you right?"

"Randy, you chose the direction of your life—I didn't force you into it. You managed to convince yourself that something was going on between Midnight and me so you could walk out on me. You were wrong, it's that simple. Now whether you believe it or not, it's not my place to prove it. You have to make your own decisions and live your own life. Just make sure you're the one who's in charge, not the guy you're screwing or the broad you're living with."

Randy was taken aback by his harsh words. He didn't usually use such crude terms around her. She hadn't realized until that moment how differently he had always treated her. She'd never heard the vulgarity he was capable of; he'd always treated her like a lady. And a child, she thought angrily.

"I see," she said. "So now you get Midnight, which is probably what you wanted all along anyway."

Joe shook his head, disbelief evident on his face. "I think that Jess is right. You're seeing what you want to see, so you can justify your own actions."

"Who's Jess?" Randy asked, grabbing at straws, starting to realize that the house of cards she had built her rebellion on was falling apart fast.

"She's a police officer up in Sacramento. She helped out at the academy class I was teaching."

"I see," Randy said, in a way that indicated what she thought Jessica had helped out with.

Joe gave her a disgusted look. "You know, Randy, those people you're hangin' out with are turning you into a real bitch."

"No," Randy countered, "they've just made me open my eyes to reality, and shown me that my knight in shining armor is no more than a normal man on a mule." Her eyes were flashing then, and Joe couldn't even imagine who she was anymore.

Shaking his head, he stood up and walked out of the room. Randy sat on the bed, trying desperately to hang on to her anger, but the tears came unbidden to her eyes. She was mad at herself, she was mad at Dick, she was even mad at Sarah for all the shit they'd been telling her. She had wanted to believe it—Joe was right. She had almost been desperate to believe what they had told her. It seemed to make sense at the time. Joe had slept with Midnight after all, she reminded herself—but it had been after the fact. She wondered then if her misplaced anger had been caused by her guilt. She wasn't sure if Midnight had been telling the truth when she claimed she didn't remember what had happened to her. Randy couldn't see a reason why she would lie. Maybe her nasty look at Randy had just been anger over Joe and her being together. Randy knew she was in a really bad spot, but she didn't know what to do to stop it.

Eventually, Joe came back into the room. Randy was still facing the headboard, so he didn't see the tears in her eyes. When she heard him, she hastily wiped them away.

"Let's go, I want to get back to the hospital," he said, his voice emotionless. Randy wanted to try to talk to him again, but one look at his face told her he was in no mood to listen to any more of her explanations. In retrospect, she couldn't exactly blame him.

The ride back to the hospital was quiet, much like the ride to the house had been, but this time it was more of a hostile silence. When they arrived, Joe got out of the car and walked inside without a glance back. Randy stood staring after him, knowing she had just gone leagues in the exact opposite direction that she had hoped to go that afternoon.

She got into Sarah's Camaro and drove off, heading back to the apartment. Her mind whirled around the conversation she'd had with Joe, trying to make sense of it. She realized she was in the wrong, but she didn't want that to be true. She kept looking for something to hold on to, to make her feel better about her decisions. She clung to the knowledge that in the end she had been right, that Joe had slept with Midnight.

CHAPTER 6

Midnight remained in the hospital, recovering from the attack that had killed her unborn child and almost taken her life. Rick was doing his best to be there for her, although she wasn't making that easy. He suspected that Midnight had known her assailant, regardless of whether or not she could remember who it was, so he wanted to be on his guard and stick close to her. He knew he'd made a lot of mistakes in the past few weeks, but that didn't mean that he didn't love his headstrong wife.

Rick had just dropped his parents off at a local hotel. They had come in from England earlier in the day, and he wanted them to rest a bit from their trip. He was just walking back into the hospital when he noticed Phil Griffin in the waiting room. Rick walked over to the head of the Bureau of Narcotic Enforcement's San Diego regional office. They shook hands, neither of them mentioning the issues that had been between them in the past few months.

"How's she doing?" Phil asked.

"You haven't seen her?" Rick said, surprised.

"No." Phil shook his head, eyeing the other man. "I thought I should wait and talk to you. I didn't want to presume too much." It was clear from Phil's voice that he knew about Rick's previous accusations about him and Midnight sleeping together.

Rick's face changed. Looking very apologetic, he said, "Look, man, I'm sorry about all that shit." He clapped Phil on the back. "You're a good friend of hers, and I know she'd want to see you. Come on."

When Rick opened the door to Midnight's room, he was surprised to see Tom Ryan sitting next to her. They were talking, and Midnight looked more alert.

Ryan glanced up at the two men as they entered the room. The look he gave Rick was measured, and Rick knew that Tom knew about what had been going on between him and Midnight. He was surprised at how uncomfortable it made him feel. Tom Ryan was like a father to Midnight, although they hadn't seen a lot of him lately, because he had finally gotten married again. After an extra moment's hesitation, Tom extended his hand to Rick. Rick took it, nodding to the older man, as if accepting his disapproval of his actions of late.

"Tom," Phil said, a frequent patron of the Pit ever since he had become acquainted with FORS and subsequently their favorite hangout.

"How ya doin?" Tom asked, his smile genuine.

"Well," Griff said, glancing over at Midnight, "I came to see our girl, see what a mess she's made out of herself this time."

"Ah yes," Tom said, as if he'd been there many times before.

Griff moved to look down at Midnight. "How're you doin, lady?"

Midnight looked up at him. She was very obviously still weak, but looked a lot better than she had only a couple of hours before. "I'll live," she said simply.

"Hey," Phil said, shaking a finger at her blasé attitude. "Listen here, missy. That's a damn sight better than you were doing last night."

"I heard," Midnight said, her voice quiet and serious.

"Well, I'm glad you're still around to be hearing anything." Phil leaned down to kiss her on the cheek. "I just wanted to stop by and see you, but I have to get back. The chief's crackin' the whip—end-of-the-year garbage is coming around."

"Thanks for coming by, Griff," Midnight said, a little stronger this time.

"Anytime." He gave her a look. "But next time, let's make it a little bit less dramatic. If you want to see me, just pick up the phone, okay?" He grinned at her, and she smiled, her humor beginning to return.

Griff left, and Tom was right behind him, telling Midnight that he would come by later that evening and check up on her.

Rick walked Tom out, knowing the older man wanted to have words with him. He steeled himself for the berating he was sure was to come.

Once out in the corridor, Tom turned to him. "So what's the deal?" he said, getting straight to the heart of the matter.

"With what?" Rick asked, not sure what part he was indicating.

"Are you done with your little fling?" Tom said coldly.

"Now wait a minute, Tom—"

"Don't 'wait a minute' me, young man, and don't try to tell me that she slept with Joe so that makes it even, because you and I both know that it doesn't." Tom's voice left no room for argument, and

Rick found himself nodding numbly. The thought had occurred to him earlier; he just hadn't been willing to examine it too closely.

Tom pointed Rick. "What's important now," he continued, sounding very much like a father, "is that you get your shit together. Now, when Midnight needs you."

"What if she won't let me be there for her?" Rick asked. His voice held no anger, only somber insight.

Tom shrugged. "That's gonna have to be something you're going to have to deal with. See, to her way of thinking, you betrayed her trust, and that's something that she may not forgive ever. But the question is, will she be willing to put it behind her and move on with you?"

Rick closed his eyes, nodding. He had thought the same thing. He had known, somewhere in the back of his mind, that screwing around on Midnight was the one thing that would surely break them up. At the time, he hadn't thought he really cared. Now he realized that he did care, very much, but it might be a moot point.

"Thanks, Tom," he said, extending his hand. "I can always count on you to give it to me straight."

"I worry about the kid," Tom said, by way of explaining his forthright behavior. "I still tend to think that her parents' rejection of her is still eating at her. I heard they were here last night, and had called about her today, so maybe. Who knows." He shrugged.

Tom left, and Rick returned to the room. When he walked in, he saw that Midnight was staring off into space. It was obvious she was thinking about something, and he could see a real conflict in her. When she noticed that he'd come in, she looked away, schooling her features. He knew he wasn't in a place to ask her too much about anything. He didn't want to push, but Tom's words kept eating at him, as did another question.

"Midnight," he said cautiously. The doctors had told him not to upset her.

She looked at him. It disconcerted him that she hadn't really said anything directly to him since she'd regained consciousness. It was like she was tolerating his presence, and that really bothered him.

"Why didn't you tell me?" he asked softly, with no real accusation, though he could tell she could see it in his eyes.

Midnight considered the question for a few moments, then looked him straight in the eye. "What would you have said?" Her voice was calm.

Rick considered the question. "Probably that you shouldn't have it," he answered honestly.

Midnight's eyes took on a knowing look, and she nodded.

"What did Joe say when you told him?" Rick asked, anger creeping into his voice.

"Same thing."

"So why am I the bastard?"

"I never said that."

"But that's why you didn't tell me, right? Because you thought I'd be a bastard and try and make you have it, or what?"

Midnight looked at him for a long time, as if she were trying to understand his way of thinking. "Actually, quite the opposite. I was sure that you and Joe would railroad me into an abortion."

"So why would that have been wrong? It could have killed you." It was as if she had forgotten or something. He was very confused now. She thought he'd want her to have an abortion, which he figured would have been a given considering her medical history with pregnancy, but somehow he was still wrong.

Midnight looked away, as if trying to hide something from him. He reached over and turned her face back to his. "Answer me," he said firmly. He wanted to understand, but he thought she was just being evasive. In a way she was, but not for the reasons he was thinking.

"I wanted the baby, okay?" Midnight said finally, angry now.

"Why?" Rick asked, totally perplexed.

Midnight shook her head, exasperated with his imperceptive mind. She really didn't want to have to explain, but it was obvious he wasn't going to leave her alone until she did.

"Because it was yours," she said stridently.

"I know that, but what difference does that make?"

"God, you can be so dumb sometimes," Midnight said, showing her irritation at being interrogated about something that she'd just as soon not discuss.

"Okay." Rick nodded. "So I'm dumb. You enlighten me then."

"No, forget it. It doesn't matter now anyway." She turned her head away from him and closed her eyes. The discussion was over.

Rick got up and walked out of the room. He paced the corridor for a while, and finally sat down on the couch in the hallway.

That was where Joe found him three and a half hours later.

"What?" Joe said, walking up to the couch.

Rick looked up at him. "Nothin'. She's fine. I just came out here to breathe."

"Breathe?" Joe raised an eyebrow.

"Sit down for a minute," Rick said with a resigned sigh. Joe complied, looking over at his friend and wondering if they were about to talk about his and Midnight's dalliance in Sacramento. "When did Midnight tell you she was pregnant?" Rick asked, no anger evident in his voice.

"Last week," Joe said. He sounded like he was on the witness stand. He thought of a motto cops used when they talked about court. "Never give them more information than they ask for."

"And what did you say?" Rick asked, again with no hint of accusation or anger.

"I told her that I'd go with her to have the abortion if she didn't want you there."

Rick visibly flinched at the mention of his absence at such a critical time. "Okay," he said, trying to keep on track. "What did she say to that?"

"She told me she was keeping it." Joe looked at Rick warily, not sure what the man was getting at.

Rick turned to him. "That's it, right there."

"That's what, right where?" Joe was sure Rick was going off-kilter from a lack of sleep.

"Why would she keep the baby if she knew it could endanger her life?" Rick was so sure Joe would agree wholeheartedly with him that he just about fell over when Joe replied.

"Because it was yours." Joe had the same look on his face that Midnight had had, as if Rick were dull-witted.

"Do you two read off the same script or what?" Rick yelled, his voice almost shrill. "What the fuck does that matter!"

Joe looked at his best friend of many years, wondering if he should call in the white coats or have the man's brain pan-tapped. Maybe all of his brain fluid had been drained by the Thelands. "Rick," he said slowly, "she loves you, and that baby was maybe her last link to you. It was yours and hers—she wanted it because she couldn't have you anymore."

Rick sat and stared at Joe, all anger, upset, and angst drained away. It was a wonder he remembered to breathe. After a few minutes, Joe could see Rick mentally falling back and regrouping. It astounded Joe that what he had just told him had seemed to come as a total shock. He realized how easy it must be to convince oneself that someone you dearly loved didn't love you anymore. He wondered if that was what Randy was trying to do—convince herself that he didn't or couldn't love her anymore.

Rick stood up and walked down the hallway. Reaching the end, he turned around, his stride speeding up as he walked back toward Midnight's room. Joe stood up, knowing what Rick was planning to do and that it wasn't a good idea.

"Rick," he said, blocking the other man's path. "Don't be fool enough to go in there and confront her with this."

"Why not?" Rick asked truculently.

"Jesus, you really don't know her, do you?" Joe was ever astonished today by his friend's obtuse frame of mind. "She'll deny everything first, then she'll get mad and have you tossed out on your ear.

You can't confront her about direct feelings—she's not the usual touchy-feely type of woman. You should know that by now. She doesn't talk about how she feels, she shows you, and that's what she was doing by keeping your baby."

Rick nodded slowly. "You're right, and I know it, but what can I do? I've screwed things up so badly with her, and now I find out that she still loved me all the same, and I can't do anything?" His voice railed at the fates for putting him in this place.

"I'll tell you what I told Randy earlier. You made the decisions, you chose your path—now you have to live with the consequences. All betrayals stand, you know."

"But what about you?" Rick asked, and Joe wondered if he would be wise to step back before Rick took a swing at him.

"What about me?" he said, his senses alert for any sort of attack.

"Where do you and her stand?"

Joe shrugged. "Got me. I told her that I wanted her and Mikeyla to stay with me, when she was pregnant." He shrugged again. "And if she doesn't take your sorry ass back, I guess I'll have to drag her kicking and screaming to my house while she recovers when she gets out of here." His voice was matter-of-fact, with a touch of humor at the end. Rick narrowed his eyes at him, and Joe was sure he was about to have to defend himself. Rick surprised him by breaking into a slow smile.

"Never am gonna understand the two of you, am I?"

"Probably not," Joe acquiesced. He knew at that moment that Rick and he had just surmounted the largest obstacle their friendship had ever encountered.

****

Randy had gone back to the apartment the evening after confronting Joe about Midnight and finding out that he had indeed slept with her, but not until after Randy had betrayed him with Dick. She proceeded to get drunk and tell Sarah everything that had been said between Joe and herself that day. Sarah was pissed at her for even going to his "beck and call."

"You don't understand," Randy had said, her eyes welling with tears. "I still love him."

"Oh, I understand," Sarah said. "I understand that you're a poor little shy girl who was rescued from her meek existence by a shining knight on a white horse, and now you're willing to let him do anything he wants to you, and anyone else he sees fit to do it to. You are so dumb, Randy. You've got a chance at someone as great as Dick, and instead you run back to that man."

Randy stared at Sarah, thinking she could tell her a thing or two about "someone great like Dick." And in her drunken state she almost did, but she stopped herself at the last minute and went off to bed.

The next morning Sarah had been curt to her, and quiet on the drive to the academy. Randy had a nasty headache and felt nowhere near well enough to go to class, but today was a lecture day, so she figured she'd be okay.

They were told that Midnight Chevalier was going to be fine. Randy felt relieved. She was at least able to pay better attention during the lecture, thinking that somehow the gods had smiled on her and let her off easy. She was feeling almost happy by lunchtime.

She and Sarah were sitting at one of the outdoor tables, talking about what lecture notes they had gotten. Suddenly, as if it were some sort of omen, a shadow fell over Randy from behind. She turned, looking up. It was the academy sergeant.

She jumped to her feet, standing at attention. She prayed this was just a snap inspection, like the ones she'd heard he conducted sometimes when cadets were relaxing.

"You have a message, cadet," the sergeant barked. "Report to the administrative office to receive it."

Randy felt her stomach tighten. She walked to the office. One of the secretaries retrieved the message, smiling as she handed it to her. Randy returned the smile, but almost gagged a moment later when she saw who the message was from. Lieutenant Midnight Chevalier wanted to see her, today. The word "today" was underlined. Randy spent the rest of the day on pins and needles. She had Sarah drop her off at the hospital, telling her she would find a way home. Then, as if she were going to her own funeral, Randy walked inside and headed toward Midnight's room.

At the door, she took a deep breath and knocked.

"Come," Midnight's voice rang out. Obviously she'd regained some of her strength, Randy thought absently as she pushed the door open. Midnight was sitting up in bed, and when Randy walked in, her eyes seemed to turn to ice.

Randy couldn't think of anything to say, so she just stood by the door, staring dumbly at the woman who had been her boss.

"Come in, Randy," Midnight said, her voice low and business-like. "I know you're not shy anymore."

159

Randy walked toward her, mustering up the courage to look her in the eye. "You wanted to see me?" she said, keeping her tone as even as she could.

"Oh yes," Midnight said, her eyes glittering maliciously.

"Look—" Randy said, trying to dissuade her nervousness by heading Midnight off.

"Save it." Midnight's voice cut through Randy's like a hot knife through butter. "You and your boyfriend did a pretty good job," she said, stunning Randy into remaining silent. "I mean, if you were trying to kill me…" She shrugged. "Okay, maybe not so good, but if you just wanted to do some damage…" She looked down, her hand resting on her stomach, then back up at Randy. The look in her eyes made Randy's entire body go cold. "Then I'd say you two did one hell of a job."

"Midnight, I had no idea—"

"Shut the fuck up, Randy," Midnight snapped, her voice pure hatred. "I don't want to hear your bullshit excuses. If it were just me and you right now, I swear you'd be dead on that floor." She laughed hollowly, a nasty, angry sound in the quiet room. "And don't fool yourself into thinking that I couldn't do it even now. What you got at the academy was just a sample."

"What do you want from me?" Randy asked, feeling very nervous. She didn't doubt Midnight's words. Right now, Midnight was not Lieutenant Chevalier with the psychology degree and the law degree; she was a gang leader, and Randy was her opponent.

"Well, see," Midnight said, her eyes narrowing, "that's the thing. I'd like to see nothing more than your ass getting thrown in jail. Have you covered attempted murder in the academy yet? How about attempted murder of a police officer? Do you know how much time you get for charges like that, Randy? And maybe you haven't had an opportunity to visit a real prison yet, but believe me, someone like you would pray to be killed, just so the rapes and beatings would end. Women inmates can be more dangerous than men in a lot of ways." Midnight's voice had taken on an informative tone. "But I have a problem."

"What's that?" Randy asked, trying desperately to muster some sort of nerve.

"Well, it seems as though for some jaded reason, my partner still loves you, and while the idea of him putting up with your cheating, lying bullshit makes me sick, I can't see myself having you put away just yet."

"So what does this mean?"

"It means that you better get your shit together and decide where your loyalties lie," Midnight said, satisfied that she'd scared the hell out of her.

Randy nodded, turning to leave.

"And Randy," Midnight said, as if she'd just had another thought. Randy turned and was shocked to see a mask of sheer determination on Midnight's face. "Tell your boyfriend I owe him one." She waved a hand at the bruises on her face. "And I always pay my debts." Midnight's voice was ruthless, and Randy knew that neither the law nor any person would stop her repaying Dick for his brutality. Randy found herself glad that she wasn't included in that threat.

Outside the hospital, Randy sat down on a bench. She was shaking from head to toe. Her face in her hands, she began to cry. Her life was spinning out of control, and she didn't seem to be capable of stopping it. After a few minutes, she walked over to a pay phone and called for a cab to La Jolla beach.

Randy Curtis-Sinclair spent the next four hours walking up and down the beach, mile after mile, trying to sort out her life.

She thought about growing up, her parents leaving, Darrell's efforts to keep their family together. She thought of meeting Midnight and being so impressed with the woman that she eventually decided she wanted to be like her. *Some rendition I turned out to be.* She thought of her time with FORS and how she had felt part of something important. She thought about wanting to be more involved, making more of a difference.

She had thought that the academy was a logical choice. But then she had taken up with Sarah, who seemed to hate men as a rule, although she dated them and used them. Sarah had hated Joe on sight. She hated his money, she hated his life, she hated the fact that he seemed to have everything, including Randy. She had started harping on Joe from the first moment she had met Randy. It had been very subtle at first, but later it had become out and out slander. Randy had been hurt by Joe's rejection of her idea to become a police officer, and Sarah had nursed that pain and turned it into loathing.

Then there was Dick. He too had hated Joe from the minute he'd met Randy. She wondered how much Dick had known about Joe before he had met her; she wondered if Dick had told Sarah about Joe before she and Sarah had even met. She looked back over her conversations with her husband, including the one that afternoon. He had already accepted the fact that she was becoming a cop—he had referred to her as part of "we." She'd forgotten about that in all that had followed. She had been so set on finding something wrong with Joe that when he gave her a perfect chance to say "I told you so," she'd done it in spades.

Joe had reminded her that she knew about his and Midnight's strange relationship before they were married, and it was true. She had seen the way the two came together in emotionally turbulent times. In fact, she realized, that was what had drawn her to Joe and Midnight. The fact that they were there for each other through thick and thin. She remembered the fights they'd had about Midnight not having backup, or the time Joe had just about raped Midnight in drunken anger when his aunt accused him of murdering his parents. He had told her everything. He had bared his soul to her, his fears, his pains. She had been the one to tell him that he needed to forgive himself for all the things that he punished himself for, and yet she had not let him forget. Not now, not when she was angry and looking for someone to blame. She had turned everything around on him, even the thing he cherished most—Midnight's friendship.

The thing he cherished most next to Randy, he had said. He had cherished her more than a seven-year friendship with Midnight, and yet she had used that friendship to hurt him, to accuse him. She'd even let her hatred flow to Midnight; it had allowed her to go to Midnight's house and let Dick do what he had done. And now... Randy sat down on the sand, her tears flowing freely. The cold wind almost cut through her, but she didn't feel it. All she could think, over and over, was that she had helped to kill Midnight's baby, almost even Midnight herself.

Midnight, who had taken the time to sit next to her in the lobby of FORS' offices and interview her in a totally casual manner, not letting on the whole time that she was Lieutenant Chevalier. The woman who had basically changed her life, who had not only

163

introduced her to Joe but had encouraged their relationship. Midnight had done so much for her, and in return Randy had stood by to witness what Dick had done. It was sickening.

"I am so fucking stupid!" she shouted into the wind.

"Sure are," came Joe's voice from behind her. Randy almost jumped out of her skin. She leapt to her feet, whirling to look at him. He was grinning down at her. He had no idea what she'd been going through for the last four hours.

"How?" Randy asked, but she looked behind him and saw the lights of their house. She had subconsciously wandered back to what she had always considered home.

"You are crazy!" Joe said, shaking his head. "You're gonna catch pneumonia out here."

Randy looked up at him. He was wearing jeans and a sweatshirt, and a slow grin spread across her face. "Look who's talking. I'll lay odds that you were sitting right over there on the deck. And," she continued, wagging her finger at him, "I'll even go so far as to bet that you were drinking again."

Joe held up his hands, as if to surrender. "You got me."

He held out his hand to her, and not hesitating even a fraction of a second, she took it. They walked up to the house. On the deck, Randy reached over and picked up a half-empty bottle of tequila. She raised an eyebrow at him. "Weren't out here too long, I see."

Joe grinned at her again and led her into the house. He turned to look down at her, concern clouding his features immediately. "Randy! Jesus, what happened?" he exclaimed, alarmed to note that she'd been doing a fair amount of crying. His hands cupped her face gently as his eyes scanned hers.

Randy reached up, taking hold of his hands. "I'm okay."

She turned and led him to the couch in the living room. She sat, pulling him down with her, once again taking both of his hands in hers and smiling up at him. "I love you, Joseph Michael Sinclair, and nothing is ever going to change that. And I won't ever be stupid enough to let you go again. If you'll take me back, that is."

Joe hesitated, surprised at her words. He wasn't sure what had transpired to make Randy do a complete one-eighty—but then he realized that he really didn't care. Randy could see him relax even as he smiled. "I think that can be arranged," he softly, but his blue eyes reflected his restraint.

Randy hugged him, then got up and went into the kitchen. She returned with a bottle of wine and, conveniently, one glass, just like she had a couple of nights before. Joe looked at the glass, raising an eyebrow.

"Can you imagine," Randy said, her voice filled with wonder. "All of the other glasses were dirty."

"Well," Joe said, smiling, "I guess we'll just have to share it then."

They drank wine together and eventually turned on the television, not ready to talk just yet. Randy found herself leaning comfortably against the man she loved, watching movies and comedy shows. They stayed up late, laughing. Randy even cried at a particularly sad movie, and she was comforted by Joe's fingers tenderly wiping the tears away.

Later they went to the bedroom, but ended up simply lying together on the bed and falling asleep, Joe's hand resting lightly on Randy's waist. Things were different at the moment, but Randy accepted that everything would need to go at Joe's pace. She was simply happy that he was willing to take her back after everything that had happened.

She woke the next morning feeling like everything in the world was right again.

It was the weekend, and she was off from school. She got out of bed carefully; Joe stirred but didn't get up. Randy put on his FORS jacket, picked up the keys to the older-model black Jaguar, and went down to the bakery in town. She came back and made coffee, which she carried in to Joe along with some fresh croissants.

Joe was already up and in the shower. Randy found herself watching him a little while later as he shaved. It was as if she were falling in love with him all over again. Suddenly, every move he made, every look, every sound, every gesture seemed new and exciting to her again. While she wanted their relationship to get back on track, especially in the intimacy department, she was determined to respect what he had told her about Midnight.

Later that morning, Randy told Joe she had something she needed to do. He didn't question her, and she was glad, not wanting to have to lie or be evasive with him. She drove the black Jaguar to the hospital and headed straight to Midnight's room. Steeling herself, she went in. Midnight was awake, and not surprisingly she was reading some sort of report.

"That didn't take long," Randy said, feeling too happy to try to be clever or sly.

Midnight looked up at Randy and was totally stunned by the change in the younger woman, so much so that she didn't speak. Randy moved over to the side of the bed.

"Midnight," she said. She spoke softly but was determined to say her piece. "You were right about everything. I have been criminally stupid, and I am so sorry. Please." She reached out to touch Midnight's arm gently. "Please know that I never meant for what happened with Dick to happen. I know," she said, seeing the look in Midnight's eyes, "that that doesn't excuse it, but I had no idea that Dick was going to do that. If anything, I figured I might get lucky and land one punch. I never even thought he'd get involved." Her eyes pleaded with Midnight to at least understand, if she couldn't forgive her. Midnight was looking at her, but her face showed no real emotion. Randy was relieved, however, to note that the hate and naked anger she'd seen the day before weren't in her eyes either. "I want you to know that I'm moving out of the apartment with Sarah, and I'm not planning to ever see Dick Dickerson again. I did exactly what you told me to, and I realized a lot of things, not least of which was how much I owe you."

Midnight narrowed her eyes slightly. "What about Joe?" she asked, her voice controlled.

"Well," Randy said, "that's actually up to you." She smiled at Midnight's surprised expression. "Joe told me about the two of you getting together in Sacramento." She spoke without a trace of anger, and Midnight was further surprised. "He told me that he had promised you that he'd be there for you. And, well, now he's waiting to see if you're going to need him."

"And if I do?" Midnight asked, wanting to cover all of the bases.

"Then he's yours," Randy said, shrugging. "You two have to be there for each other—that's what makes you who you are. I've regained my understanding of that now. I'll wait for him, though, because I've also regained my senses, and I remember now that Joe is the best thing that's ever happened to me."

Midnight gave her a measured look. "If you ever hurt him again, I swear I'll kick your ass."

Randy nodded, her expression serious. "If I ever hurt him again, I expect you to." The two women stared at each other, both of them wondering what would happen.

"And what's goin' on in here?" Rick asked from the door. Midnight and Randy glanced over at him, then looked back at each other and laughed.

Rick watched them both for a moment, an odd grin on his face. He knew he had missed something. He felt a tug at his leg and looked over at Midnight. "I have someone here that wants to see you." He stepped back.

A tiny, copper-blond-haired blur ran into the room, squealing with delight as she threw herself toward her mother. "Mikeyla!" Rick called firmly. The child stopped just short of the bed and looked back at her father. "Remember what we talked about. Mommy is still hurt, so you have to be careful, okay?" Mikeyla nodded, her eyes wide as she turned back to look at her mother, very obviously trying to determine where her mommy's "boo-boo" was. She looked up at Randy and smiled sweetly as she held up her arms to her.

Randy bent down and picked the girl up, then looked at Midnight.

"Go ahead and set her here." Midnight patted her lap.

Randy hesitated, looking over at Rick. He shrugged, knowing arguing with Midnight about this would be pointless. Randy did as she was asked. Mikeyla immediately leaned her head down against Midnight's chest, having very apparently missed her mother a great deal. Midnight wrapped her arms around her daughter, holding her close. Randy was always amazed at the change in Midnight's face when she was with Mikeyla. It made Randy feel like she was missing something very important in her life.

"I'd better be going," Randy said, knowing she should get out of the way.

Midnight looked up at her for a long moment, her eyes searching the younger woman's. Randy didn't look away. She knew Midnight was trying to see if there was any type of deception, and it made Randy all the more aware of the change her personality had undergone in the past month or so. Midnight would never have had to look at her in that way before. Finally, Midnight smiled a half-smile, pleased with what she'd seen in Randy's face—and also in Randy's direct gaze, which went a long way to proving to Midnight that Randy's words had been sincere.

Randy left, closing the door slowly behind her. Rick stood still, close to the door. He had watched the exchange, and he knew that something very important had occurred between the two women, and he was very curious about what that was. He also knew that asking Midnight a battery of questions would get him into yet another battle, and he wasn't there for that.

Mikeyla sat back on Midnight's lap, looking at her mother. "When can you come home?" she asked, getting straight to the important matter at hand.

"I don't know, sweetie," Midnight said. "The doctors want to keep me here long enough to make sure I'm okay first."

Again Mikeyla looked up at her mother intently. She reached up, delicately touching the bruise on the side of Midnight's face. "Is this your boo-boo, Mommy?"

Midnight nodded.

"How did you get it?"

Midnight looked up at Rick, and then back at her daughter. "Mommy's not exactly sure," she said, and from the tone of her voice and her hesitation, Rick could tell instantly that she was lying. She didn't like to lie to Mikeyla, and Rick knew that the circumstances would have to be extreme for her to do so. He recognized that he was due to have another argument with Midnight, because this was too important to let go.

He watched Mikeyla and Midnight visit for about a half hour, then told Mikeyla she needed to go with Grandma and Grandpa while he and Mommy talked. Mikeyla was reluctant to leave, but she knew better than to argue with her father.

Midnight knew what was coming. She knew Rick was aware that she had lied. She also wasn't sure how she was going to get out of this. The moment Mikeyla left, Rick walked over to the bed.

He looked down at her, his eyes narrowed slightly, not in anger but in analysis. He was trying to figure out what she was doing.

"Okay," he said simply. "Explain."

Midnight considered playing dumb, but she knew it would be a waste of time. Rick was like a pit bull when it came to things like this.

"Look," she said, trying to put more confidence in her voice than she could really muster. "I told you what I did to keep some things from happening."

"And?" Rick prompted, not willing to be put off that easily.

"And," Midnight said, "I'm still not ready to talk about it, okay?"

"No, it's not okay." Rick was exasperated at her evasiveness. "Tell me what the fuck is going on, Midnight."

"Rick, I can't, okay?" Midnight said, her voice taking on a desperate edge.

"Why?" He sounded almost hurt.

Midnight closed her eyes, not wanting to lie to him too. "If I tell you right now, it could hurt someone else, and I'm not ready to do that just yet."

"Who's it gonna hurt?" Rick asked, looking very confused. "Why are you protecting the person that almost killed you and who did kill our baby?"

Tears came to Midnight's eyes, but her face contorted into a mask of anger and vengeance. "Don't worry, I'll take care of him myself." Her voice was rough with frustration and fury.

Rick looked alarmed. "I don't want you taking care of anyone by yourself. This is my fight too."

Midnight looked up at him sharply, surprised that he suddenly seemed to care about the baby that he originally thought she should have gotten rid of.

Rick noticed her surprise and shrugged self-consciously. "Let's just say that someone set me straight on that one, okay?" Midnight suspected she knew just who that someone was. Joe did have a tendency to talk out of turn.

"Okay," she said, unwilling to continue the discussion further. Fortunately, there was a knock at the door. "Come," Midnight called, before Rick could tell the person to go away. She was sorry a moment later when her parents walked hesitantly into the room. Midnight's eyes flashed angrily as she looked up at Rick. "What are they doing here?" she said, not caring if they heard.

"Midnight." Rick was surprised at her tactlessness. "I had them called," he said, trying to end the conversation quickly. Carrie and Jack were standing still at the door, but it was obvious they were as uncomfortable as Rick.

"I see." Midnight looked at her parents. She saw before her the people who had not only disregarded her as a child but had only become interested in her life when Thomas died, and only so much as to accuse her of causing his death. They had shunned her from that day on. Now here they were, standing in her hospital room, looking at her like she was their daughter again. She noted their discomfort as well, and she was determined not to alleviate their feelings. Midnight tilted her head to the side, as if not recognizing them. "You looking for someone?" she said caustically.

Carrie looked up at her husband, and when she saw no support from that area, she glanced over to Rick. Rick said nothing, not wanting to make things worse. He knew they needed to work through this. He stepped back, moving to sit in a chair by the wall. He gave Midnight a look as if to say, "You're on your own."

"Midnight," Carrie said. The name of her own child sounded strange to her, she uttered it so rarely. "We wanted to be here." Her voice was so hesitant that Midnight wanted to laugh. Here was her mother, saying one thing with her mouth and something totally different with her heart.

"Yeah," she said scornfully. "I can tell."

"You don't need to speak to your mother that way," Jack put in sternly. And this time Midnight did laugh.

"What, are you kidding?" she said, her voice dripping with sarcasm. "Since when is that woman my mother?" She pointed to Carrie, her voice and eyes turning to ice as she looked at her father. "And who the hell are you to tell me what not to do?"

"Whether you like it or not, Midnight Katherine Chevalier, I am your father, and—"

"Katherine?" Midnight exclaimed. "What the hell is that?"

Jack shook his head, as if not understanding her question.

"Who's Katherine?" Midnight asked, her voice indicating that she didn't believe his ignorance.

"You are," Carrie said. "Midnight Katherine Chevalier—you were named after my favorite sister."

Midnight stared at this woman, her mother, and couldn't even begin to think of a response. She had never heard the name before; she had always assumed she didn't have a middle name. She certainly hadn't ever seen a birth certificate, and no one in school had ever gotten past the peculiarity of her first name and the difficulty of pronouncing her last name.

"I have an aunt?" she asked finally, dumbfounded.

Carrie nodded. "Yes. She lives in Ireland. That's where my part of the family is from, Midnight." She was speaking patiently, as if to a small child, and Midnight didn't like it.

"I know that I'm part Irish, okay. But I didn't know that you had a sister. I guess I don't know too much about either of you, since you never bothered to talk to me. Except, of course, to tell me that I killed your one and only son." Midnight's voice was strained. She looked away from her parents, not wanting them to see the hurt in her eyes.

Carrie took a couple of steps to stand next to Midnight's bed. She reached over to touch her daughter's hand. Midnight snatched it away, looking at her mother as if she couldn't believe the woman's nerve. In truth, she couldn't. She glared at Rick, feeling like he had betrayed her by calling her parents.

"Maybe the three of us getting to know each other wouldn't be a bad thing," Carrie said hopefully.

"Why?" Midnight said. "So you can tell me in a hundred different ways what a disappointment I am, and how if it wasn't for me your baby son would still be alive for you to ignore?"

"Are you denying that it was because he was in the gang that he was killed?" Jack Chevalier said, his voice taking on the familiar tone.

"You know," Midnight said, reaching up to snatch the IV from her arm as she got out of bed, "I don't need this shit."

Rick stood up and stepped toward her, but she gave him an icy stare that stopped him. She looked up at her father. He stood a good seven inches taller than her, but she didn't look the least bit inferior to him. "Listen, you stupid son of a bitch. If you or her had given a shit about me or Thomas, neither one of us would have been in the gang. But you didn't. You cared about everything else, your friends, your drinking, your TV, your dope, and whatever else you were into. So don't fucking talk to me about your son. He was my brother, and I watched him die!" There were tears in her eyes. "I sat there in the middle of the street and watched his blood seep out onto the pavement!" Her voice had risen hysterically, and Rick came to stand behind her. He was alarmed to notice that blood was pooling on the floor, dripping down her arm.

"Midnight," he said warningly.

Midnight spun around to stare up at him. "What?" she yelled, seething.

"Get back into bed," he said firmly.

Midnight glanced behind her at her parents. "Get them out of here and I'll get back in bed."

"Do it now, Midnight, or I'll pick you up and put you there myself." Rick could already see that she was weakening. Without another word, he reached out and picked her up. He was alarmed when Midnight basically passed out the moment he lifted her. He looked up at Jack, his eyes narrowed. "If you ever talk to her like that again, I'll knock you out myself. Now get the hell out of here."

Jack looked at Rick, stunned. Carrie moved to her husband, taking his arm and ushering him out of the room. A few minutes later she came back and helped Rick put Midnight into the bed.

"What the hell is wrong with you people?" Rick said disbelievingly.

"I'm sorry," Carrie said. "Jack feels like Midnight is at fault, and no amount of talking will change his mind, I'm afraid."

"You don't think that though?" he said, surprised. She had seemed convinced, that time he visited them with Mikeyla.

Carrie shook her head ruefully. "No, it's just easier with Jack sometimes to agree with him. I used to think it was her fault. She surprised Rick further by reaching up to brush a copper-gold lock of hair from her daughter's face. "But I realize now that I was just trying to hide my guilt in accusation."

"Well," Rick said, still angry with them for upsetting Midnight, "it would have been nice for her to know that at least you didn't really blame her."

"She knows it wasn't her fault."

Rick stared at her for a long moment. "You don't really believe that?"

Carrie blinked, the look in her eyes indicating that yes, she really did.

"God." Rick rolled his eyes. "Midnight has blamed herself every day since his funeral, and you two blaming her just set it in concrete for her. You're her parents, for God's sake!" Carrie just looked at him blankly, and he growled with exasperation. "Don't you know what that did to her? If her own parents think Thomas' death was her fault, what do you think she's gonna think?"

"I guess I never really thought about it that way."

"Think about it."

The nurse came in, responding to Rick's page, and Carrie left the room a few minutes later. Rick leaned back in the chair he had been sitting in for so many hours. He watched Midnight, thinking about all that she'd been through in her life. It didn't seem fair. He had always had it so good—a family that adored him, who he adored, just about anything he'd ever wanted. His parents had supported him, no matter what. And yet, Midnight had accomplished so much.

Rick had fallen asleep as he sat thinking about everything. He was awoken by a knock on the door. He got up and walked over to open it. He was shocked to find himself staring at Sheila Theland.

"What are you doing here?" he said, a hint of anger in his voice.

"I haven't seen you. I just—"

"Sheila! This is hardly the time or the place."

"Well… when, where?"

Rick realized she had no idea that it was over between them. "Sheila," he said tiredly. He didn't want to handle this right now. "Later, okay? I'll call you."

"Okay," she said, and surprised him by reaching up to kiss him. Rick moved his face so she only kissed his cheek; he basically pushed her away after that. She didn't seem to notice his brusque treatment. Shaking his head, he watched her walk away down the hall.

****

When Randy got back to the house, she found Joe lying on one of the lounge chairs out on the deck. She felt a little bit better after her conversation with Midnight, but she knew she was still keeping something from Joe. She also knew that to tell him now would be more than counterproductive to any type of reconciliation. Looking down at him, she saw that he was asleep. He was exhausted from all of the events of the last couple of days. They hadn't slept as much the night before as they should have, but they had been enjoying being together again.

Randy bent down and kissed him on the cheek softly. His eyes opened instantly. He reached up, taking her hand and pulling her down on the lounge chair with him. Randy laughed quietly as she snuggled close to him, enjoying his familiar playful side. They lay together, Randy turning so that she could rest her head on his shoulder as they both looked out over the ocean.

After an hour or so, Joe whispered to her that he thought they should move to where they'd be more comfortable, since they were both falling asleep. Randy stood up, holding Joe's hand and tugging him to his feet. She led him inside and down the hall to the bedroom. Joe lay on the bed and pulled her down with him. Randy turned on her side, her back to him, and his arms wound around her protectively. They fell asleep.

A few hours later, the phone rang, and Joe reached over sleepily to answer it.

"'Lo" he said, his accent thick from sleep.

"Joe?" came a familiar voice.

"Jess! Hey, how're you?"

"More importantly," Jessica said, her usual humor intact, "how's the lieutenant?"

"Better," Joe said, smiling. Randy was awake, and she turned over, watching him. Joe didn't notice her eyes on him; he was lying on his back, his arm still under Randy's neck, his hand shifting to hold her tight against his side. She watched as her husband talked to "Jess"; she wasn't jealous—she was curious—but she found herself looking at Joe as she had that morning, as if she were just falling in love with him all over again.

"Everyone was asking about you. They were wondering if you're coming back."

"Yeah, I know," Joe said, looking remorseful. "I just don't know at this point."

"Well, everyone at the academy voted, and they don't want to graduate till you come back and finish teaching them." Jessica sounded sincere.

Joe laughed, closing his eyes. "Great. It'll be full summer by the time I can come back, and they want me to teach at an outdoor range. Don't it get to about a hundred there?" His eyes were twinkling as he said it, and Randy could tell he was trying to bait the person on the other end of the line.

"I'll personally find you a nice indoor range, Sergeant Sinclair," Jessica said, sounding very official.

"I see." Joe grinned. "Sounds to me like the class ain't the only ones voting to get me back there." There was no vanity in his statement, only pleasure at having been appreciated that much.

"Well, that's true enough," Jessica said seriously. "Remember you promised to get me back out on the street..." She trailed off, hoping she didn't sound like she thought that him being there for Midnight was less important than a dumb little promise.

"I remember full well, young lady," Joe said sternly, with a hint of humor. "I will tell you what, though. How 'bout you come down here. I can get you ready for real streets, not those tame Sacramento streets."

"Are you offering me a job, Sergeant?" she asked, surprised.

"Maybe in the long run," Joe said, making no commitments. It was Midnight's unit, after all. "But I would like to help you get your nerve back."

Jessica laughed. "Yeah, me and my whole family, right? Maybe I should bring Gary—he sure misses Midnight."

Joe laughed with her. "I'll bet."

Jessica became quiet for a moment. "Joe," she said, much more seriously now, "how are things going with you?"

Joe knew what she was talking about, and he nodded. He glanced down at Randy and saw that she was watching him. Randy smiled, and he smiled back. "Much better," he told Jessica, his eyes on Randy's.

"Really?" Jessica remembered the state he had been in just a week before.

"Yes, really, Jess."

"So Randy and you?" Jessica said, making what she figured was a natural assumption.

Joe grinned again. "Yes, Detective."

"Oh, stop!" Jessica said, then her voice grew serious again. "I'm glad, Joe. Really."

"Thanks, Jess." Joe smiled warmly, and Jessica could almost feel it over four hundred miles away.

"I just might take you up on the offer to come down though," she said.

"Tell me when and I'll pick you up. You can stay at my place, so it won't be a major money drain."

"Won't that be inconvenient for you two?" Jessica asked, not wanting to impose.

"No, it won't. We'll take good care of you. Hell, I don't think your dad would let you come down if he thought you'd be staying in some hotel."

"Well, that's true enough, being that you are my lifesaver and all."

"God, don't start that shit again," Joe said, chagrined.

"It's true, Joe, and you know it."

"It's not, and I don't," he replied stubbornly.

"You are hopeless," Jessica said, rolling her eyes. "I just hope Randy knows what a great guy she's got." Her tone was earnest, and Joe couldn't help but smile.

"Well, if she doesn't, I'm sure you can set her straight when you get here." He spoke lightly, but Jessica didn't care. She had every intention of doing just that if the need arose. Randy Sinclair was a damn lucky lady, and Jessica found herself wishing once again that Joe had a brother.

"Damn straight," she said. "Call me when you know how you want to handle the academy."

"I will. And you call me when you decide to come out."

"You got it, boss."

"Bye, Jess," Joe said, laughing again.

Joe looked at Randy as he reached across her to hang up the phone, and realized how closely she had been watching. "What?"

A slow smile spread across Randy's face as she shook her head. "I just…" she started to say, but stopped.

"Just what?"

"I just can't get over you again." She almost felt like the shy schoolgirl she had been with him years before.

"Over me?" he said, confused.

"I find myself watching you and feeling like everything is new again."

"Interesting," Joe said, his grin mischievous. He touched her arm, stroking it thoughtfully. Randy watched as the expression on his face changed.

"What?" she said.

Joe grinned as his eyes met hers, and he leaned down and kissed her. When their lips parted, he looked into her eyes again. His hand brushed down her arm, moving to her waist. His eyes trailed down after his hand, as if he were examining the places he had just touched. He moved his hand down her thigh, then bent her leg at the knee to bring it up over his legs and ran his hand along her calf. Randy shivered at the sensations. It had been so long since they had been together—too long. Joe looked up into her eyes again, as if he were searching for something.

"What?" Randy said again, this time longing coloring her voice.

Joe heard it and grinned seductively at her. Randy suspected he had full knowledge of how he was affecting her, but she was enjoying it.

"You're different," Joe said finally.

"Different how?" Randy asked, her voice a husky whisper.

"Stronger, leaner." Joe made the words sound sexy somehow.

Randy nodded at him, and he leaned down to kiss her again. This time there was almost an electric charge between them, and Randy felt his hand moved to her shirt. As they kissed, she could feel him undoing the buttons. Her body was shaking from the anticipation. It was obvious Joe was enjoying his effect on her. She had no idea how hard he was fighting to keep control over his own body, but he was much better at hiding it than she was.

When he had finished unbuttoning her shirt, Randy sat up and pulled it off. She wore no bra. Her eyes never left Joe's as she discarded the shirt. Before she could lie down, he reached over and pulled at the button to her jeans, undoing it. Taking the suggestion, Randy stood and removed her jeans as well. Joe took her hand and pulled her back to the bed. Randy's entire body began to shake as his hands slid seductively down her arms and hips again. He took her leg again, to bring it over his own. He had made no move yet to remove his clothes. Randy didn't want to think; she just wanted to revel in the feel of his hands.

After a few minutes, he moved her to her back and leaned over her, kissing her passionately. Her hands entwined in his hair, but after a few moments he reached up and gently removed them, holding them in his own, as if telling her this was his seduction, not hers. She smiled, kissing him back and not caring what he did at this point, as long as he continued to touch her. But as her body began to demand more, Randy moved to push him back, to lean over him. Joe surprised her by taking her by the waist and pulling her over to strad-dle him.

She was surprised to realize that he had somehow managed to remove her underwear—in her frustration she hadn't even noticed. Randy looked down into his eyes and shuddered at the expression there. He was looking at her body appreciatively, as if admiring an expensive piece of art. His hands traced the line of her body from her shoulders down her arms, then slipped from her hands to her waist and up the sides of her breasts, then back down to slide along her legs, which straddled his waist. His eyes never left hers, and Randy was sure she would explode soon—her body was shaking with the barely contained passion.

Joe sat up, moving her body with his. He put his lips to her bare shoulder, kissing it gently. He continued to kiss her until his lips fi-nally, exquisitely came to rest just between her breasts. He hadn't touched her breasts up until this point, and Randy thought she'd die with the anticipation. Her hands moved to his head, holding him against her as her body seemed to come alight with a fire from within. She had never experienced such slow-burning heat before. Her body trembled and shook. Joe's hands moved over her bare back as he fi-nally kissed her breasts. His hands tightened on her skin as she cried out, her body convulsing against him. Randy felt like she had just ex-ploded into a million pieces as she grasped Joe's hair in her hands, holding his head to her, as if letting go meant the incredible sensa-tions she was feeling would stop.

Minutes later, Joe rested the side of his face against her chest. Randy stroked his hair. She could feel his breath warm against her skin, and she reveled in the sensations still coursing through her body. She understood that Joe hadn't made love to her because of what he had told her the day before. It had been his way of telling her that he wanted to, but that he couldn't until he knew what Midnight expected from him. In a way, Randy felt more pride in his dedication to a promise he had made, even if that promise kept them from being as close as they could be. She steered her thoughts away from the situation, not wanting to overthink what had just happened.

Joe lay back a while later, pulling her down with him so that she lay over his body, her head resting on his shoulder and her lips next to his jaw. She looked up at him and saw that he was watching her. A slow grin started on his face, and Randy grinned back.

"That was…" Randy started to say, her voice still showing the effects of the experience. She shook her head, not able to put it into words.

"I love you," Joe said, as if trying to make up for the fact that they hadn't actually made love. His voice was deep with emotion.

"I know." In her way, Randy was telling him that it was okay, that she understood. "I owe you though," she said, her voice taking on a new edge, and Joe was surprised by her brashness. In the three years they'd been married, they had always had good love-making, but mostly because they were so much in love. It was always tender and sweet, rarely bordering on the hot and heavy type of sex that Joe was used to with other women. He had never missed it, but now, with Randy's comment, he found himself looking forward to the payback. He clamped down on the thought that she had acquired this new way of being from Dickerson, but he didn't do it quickly enough and Randy saw the change in his expression. She sat up, eyeing him.

Joe began to shake his head, his expression indicating that he did not want to have this conversation.

"Joe," Randy said, her voice soft but strong. "We need to talk about this sometime."

"Not now, Randy, please." His own voice was very soft, his eyes pained.

Randy reached over and picked her shirt up off the floor. She shrugged into it and did up a couple of the buttons. She looked at him, shaking her head.

"If we don't talk about it, Joe, we can't get past it."

Joe knew she was right, but he wasn't sure he could handle talking about her and Dickerson. She could tell by the look in his eyes that she had inflicted a lot of pain on him with her betrayal.

"Joe?" she said cautiously, feeling the need to comfort him but aware that if she didn't know what he was thinking, she couldn't. "Talk to me."

Joe reflected that she sounded like he had over three years ago, trying to get her to talk to him. It was funny, what time could change. He looked back at her, but it was obvious he wasn't seeing her. His eyes were narrowed. "When I heard about it," he said miserably, "all I could think of was that you had always been mine, and no one else's." His eyes focused on her, and Randy thought she would die from the look of pain in them. "But that wasn't true anymore."

Randy stared at him, realizing what he had just said. It shocked her to think that she hadn't thought of it that way. Joe had been the only man she had ever been with, and now something had changed that could never be changed back. The thought hit her hard. It was yet another consequence of an action she had taken so lightly. In truth, Dickerson hadn't even come close to Joe's worst day in bed; he certainly hadn't been capable of making her feel the kind of excitement she'd felt a short while ago. She wondered if that had to do with Dick's lack of sexual prowess or if it had everything to with the fact that she deeply loved Joe. She also wondered if her renewed infatuation with her husband had allowed her to go beyond what she had been capable of feeling before.

"I'm sorry," she said, her voice breaking. There were tears in her eyes as she shook her head miserably. "God, I have been so stupid, and every moment it's like I'm finding out what else I have ruined with that stupidity." She looked at him, her eyes begging him. "Can you even begin to forgive me, Joe?" Her voice was so sincere and so despondent that Joe found it impossible not to reach out and pull her to him. He sat up, pulling her into his embrace in the same motion.

"I love you, Randy, and nothing you could do could ever change that," he said, his lips in her hair as he rocked her. She was crying now, her body wracked with sobs.

"I've been so awful." Randy's voice was muffled because her face was pressed against his shirt. "Like someone else."

"Yes, love," Joe said tenderly. His voice turned wry. "And we'll start the search for the pod later."

Randy laughed miserably, and Joe laughed too. She looked up at him, her face tear-streaked. Joe reached down and brushed the tears away with his thumb.

"We'll be just fine, baby. Don't you worry."

"But—" Randy started to say, but Joe shook his head.

"We'll be fine. I love you, and you're not getting away again." His voice was stern, and Randy nodded solemnly. "Lighten up, will ya?" Joe said, wanting her to be happy again.

"Do you want to hit me or something?"

"What?"

Randy looked up at him, a grin on her face. "I mean, if you want to, it's okay. I'd understand." She was smiling now, and Joe started to shake his head.

"No," he said. He was smiling too, but his voice was serious. "But if you ever try to leave me again, I will handcuff you to something permanently."

Randy stared at him for a moment, but he couldn't keep the straight face any longer and he started to grin. She punched him on the arm as she started to laugh. Then they were silent for a few minutes, Joe just holding her close.

"Are you going back to the hospital tonight?" Randy said eventually, her face still against Joe's chest.

"Yeah."

She looked up at him. "Would you mind if I didn't go?"

Joe considered the question, imagining that it must be difficult for her right now. He had no idea. Finally he shook his head.

"I was thinking that I should go over to the apartment," Randy said hesitantly. "Get my stuff and let Sarah know…" She trailed off, because she realized she wasn't sure what to tell Sarah. Randy herself wasn't sure what was going to happen between her and Joe, but she assumed that she was welcome back to their home.

Joe read her uncertainty and nodded. "Tell her you're coming home." He sounded strong and sure, as if there had never been a doubt in his mind that she belonged there. Randy was once again astounded by his ability to forgive.

CHAPTER 7

Midnight woke in the dim light of the hospital room, feeling like she was trying to move under a soaking wet blanket. She knew it was the painkillers they were injecting into her IV every four hours or so. As if on cue, the nurse walked in carrying the hypodermic kit for just such an administration. Midnight held up her hand and the woman halted dubiously. Rick stood from his chair and came over to the bed.

"What's wrong?" he asked.

"Nothing," Midnight said, eyeing the nurse. "That's just it. I feel fine, but they keep pumping that crap into me. I feel like I'm swimming in quicksand." She looked at Rick, her face set in a determined line. "I don't want any more."

"Ms. Chevalier," the nurse interjected, shaking her head vehemently. "I don't think you realize the extent of your injuries. Perhaps if Doctor Duhane could—"

Midnight stopped her with a look. "I don't think you realize, Nurse," she said, her voice even but bordering on anger, "that I don't like to be doped up. It's not a healthy thing in my profession."

"But—"

"You're not listening to me." Midnight made a cutting gesture with her hand. "I said no more, and that's final." She saw Rick watching her worriedly and turned to him. "Don't you start with me too."

Rick held his hands up in a gesture of surrender. "Okay, you're the boss."

Midnight nodded triumphantly, and after making a note on Midnight's chart, the nurse turned and left.

An hour later, Joe walked into the room. Midnight smiled at him.

"Hey," he said, returning the smile. "You look a lot better."

"Gee, thanks."

Joe looked around. "Where's Rick?"

"His parents dragged him off to dinner." Midnight remembered his reluctance to leave her. She'd almost gotten out of bed to help them drag him out of the room—that was when he gave up and went willingly.

"Good," Joe said, sitting down on the side of the bed. "We need to talk."

Midnight looked at him for a long moment, sure she knew what he meant. "Okay."

"What're you gonna do when they release you from here?" Joe narrowed his eyes at her slightly, as if looking for some sort of deception forming in her mind.

"I don't know just yet," she said, shrugging. Her eyes took on a humorous glint. "I was thinking about going back to work, busting bad guys, making the streets safe for women and children, all that."

Joe shook his head, knowing she had thrown the last in to try and deflect his questions. "Night," he said warningly, "you know what I mean."

Midnight sighed. "Yes, I do." She looked directly into his eyes. "You want to know if I'm going to need you."

Joe gave her a lopsided grin. "Somethin' like that."

"Well, the answer is no and yes."

"What does that mean?"

"It means, Joseph Sinclair, that no, I won't need you, and yes, I want you and Randy to get back together."

Joe gave her a measured look, pursing his lips as if trying to decide if he wanted to be offended by her rebuff. "I see," he said finally. "And you'll be taken care of by whom?"

Again Midnight sighed. "I don't know yet, Joe, but it doesn't matter. I won't let it be you." Her voice held conviction.

"And what if I don't give you a choice?" he said, equally sure of himself.

"Then I'll have to shoot you," she said sweetly, batting her eyelashes at him.

"Cute." Joe grinned, but his eyes were still somber. "Seriously, Midnight, how are you going to manage? With Mikeyla and all, I think you should consider—"

"I know what you think, Joseph Michael Sinclair, and neither that thought nor the one that will certainly follow is going to cut it right now."

"But, Night—"

"No, Joe," Midnight said harshly. "I won't take Rick back just because I had the unfortunate luck to have a miscarriage, and I certainly won't interfere with you and Randy getting back together. You got it?"

Joe looked at her for a long moment. "I got it, but I don't have to like it."

Midnight shrugged. "I suppose."

"You really piss me off sometimes, ya know."

"Well, sweetheart," Midnight said, patting his hand, "rest assured in the knowledge that your sentiment is reciprocated thoroughly."

Joe stayed a little while longer, still not happy with her obstinacy but giving up the battle for now. Midnight fell asleep shortly after he left. She woke less than an hour later, writhing in pain. She moaned quietly and heard someone in the room move toward her in response. She assumed it would be Rick, but when she looked up, she saw her mother's face.

"What're you doing here?" Midnight said, her voice strained.

Carrie shook her head. "Are you in pain?" she asked, though she already knew the answer from the way Midnight was holding her stomach.

After a moment's hesitation, Midnight nodded miserably. "It's my own fault," she said, her voice cracking as she drew in deep breaths. "I told them not to give me anything." She was shaking her head now, as if trying to will the pain away.

Carrie reached over and pushed the button for the nurse. When the nurse didn't respond quickly enough, Carrie went out into the hallway. "Excuse me," she called out authoritatively. "My daughter needs some medication."

The nurse looked up at her. "It'll be a few minutes, ma'am."

Carrie walked over to the woman, her eyes narrowed. "No, you're not listening to me. She needs medication now."

The nurse looked at her for a moment and shook her head. "You don't understand, ma'am. Ms. Chevalier turned her medication down two hours ago. I tried to warn her, but she wouldn't listen."

"I don't think you understand," Carrie said, trying to keep her voice even. "My daughter is a police officer, and she needs to keep her wits about her to do her job properly. It is her propensity to stick to that on a normal basis. However, if you know that she is in unbearable pain, it is your responsibility to override her decision if it is an uneducated one."

The nurse looked at Carrie for a long moment, obviously trying to decide if she did have some modicum of fault in all of this. She must have come to the decision that Carrie was right, because she told her she'd be right in.

Carrie walked back into Midnight's room, proud of herself for being able to think quickly enough to make the nurse feel guilty. She had no idea if what she had said had been totally true, but she'd gone by what she'd seen of Midnight and her friends so far.

She looked down at Midnight. There were tears in her daughter's eyes. Midnight refused to look at her mother; she didn't want to show the woman any weakness.

Carrie turned as the nurse walked in and administered the medication to Midnight's IV. She told Carrie that it would take approximately twenty to thirty minutes to take effect.

Carrie moved to stand next to the bed. She reached down and brushed a lock of hair away from Midnight's face. "You know, when you were about seven you had this thing for cherry chip ice cream.

You'd eat it morning, noon, and night if I'd let you." She realized that Midnight was watching her and actually listening. "One time when your father was out of town, I foolishly let you eat all the ice cream you wanted." She made a face. "You proceeded to throw up all over the place. I felt so bad for letting you overindulge. You were so sick."

"I remember that," Midnight said, surprising Carrie. "I didn't until just now. Didn't we have an avocado-colored couch?"

Carrie laughed. "Yes, we did. Cherry chip didn't match it very well, I'm afraid."

"I guess now I know why I can't stand the smell of cherries," Midnight said slowly. She was obviously still in pain, but Carrie could see that the distraction was helping.

"I was so afraid that your father would find out, I spent the whole next day cleaning it up. I had it spotless, and your father would never have known except that Thomas found it necessary to tell him the minute he walked in the door. 'Sister threw up, she ate too much ice cream!' was the first thing he said." Carrie was immediately sorry she had mentioned Thomas; she saw the look on Midnight's face change.

"Don't," Midnight said, holding up a hand to fend her mother off and shaking her head. "I don't want to talk about him."

"But Midnight, that's the reason that we've—"

"That you've hated me for so long, I know."

"No, Midnight, that's not it. We never hated you…" But Carrie trailed off as she saw the look in her daughter's eyes, and she knew that they had let Midnight think that all along. She saw now the effect it had had on her. "Midnight…" Carrie breathed. "This is so difficult."

"Difficult how, Mother?" Midnight said sarcastically. "Difficult to understand how your own daughter could kill your son, difficult to understand why your daughter didn't die instead? What's so difficult to understand—he was my brother and I let him into my gang and he got killed, so by definition I killed him, right?" There were tears in Midnight's eyes. "The thing is, you never gave a shit, neither of you. Not about me, not about Thomas, until he was dead. Suddenly you were parents again—his parents, not mine though."

"We have always been your parents," Carrie said feebly.

"Bullshit!" Midnight yelled, her eyes flashing in anger. "The last time I remember having parents was around the age of nine. After that you two didn't exist, not for me or for Thomas. I took care of him, and I watched him die. I guess it's only fair."

Carrie nodded slowly. "You're right, we weren't parents to either of you for a long time. We were caught up in so much. Midnight, there's no excuse for it, but you should know that your father and I are trying to come back from the self-induced hell we've put ourselves in. I guess a lot of it did start when you were nine. We decided that we were young and we should have some fun. We were stupid, we got into drugs and drinking, and it caught us up in a whirlwind."

Again, Midnight was shaking her head, as if telling Carrie that her excuses weren't good enough.

"Midnight, I know that this doesn't excuse anything, but when Angela Theland called me and said that you might die, I had to come. I had to see you."

"Why?" Midnight asked, her eyes narrowed suspiciously.

"I've been wanting to talk to you for so long, to tell you how sorry I am about everything that we've done. But I was afraid."

Midnight raised an eyebrow, indicating that she didn't believe her.

"I was, Midnight. I was afraid of what you'd say, even of what you'd do. When that boy died four years ago, when we saw the pictures of you, you looked so devastated, it reminded me of Thomas' funeral, and I wanted to call you." She shrugged. "But your father told me he would call, because he didn't want you to scream at me. And I know he handled it badly, bringing up Thomas again. I was so angry at him for so long after that. But I just couldn't face you."

Midnight looked as if she was considering the things that Carrie was saying. She remembered now that she had been a good mother for the first nine years. She had been attentive and fun. That had made it all the more difficult when Carrie seemed to change overnight and was constantly pushing her away. Midnight remembered all the nights she had lain in her bed crying, wondering what she had done to make her mother stop loving her. Thomas had felt the same way, and Midnight had nursed her own wounds by taking care of him and giving him the love that her parents didn't seem to want anymore.

"When I came here, to see you at the hospital, and I saw all the people that you had touched, I was astounded. I talked to some of the members of your unit, and they just talked on and on about all the things you had done, and how you'd turned them around and made them respectable people again. And then the men in your life, they seem to care so much for you, it's incredible, and I began to realize what a special person it took to be able to be so much to so many people. To be loved by so many people."

"Except my own parents," Midnight said darkly.

"Midnight—" Carrie began, tears in her eyes now.

"You can't change who I am, Carrie. It was your rejection that made me who I am. It was the idea that my own parents didn't want me that made me take in everyone else. But it made me cautious too, sometimes too cautious. But that's me, a product of my environment and a will to survive."

Carrie studied her daughter for a long moment. "So I guess that degree in psychology I heard about is true, huh?"

Midnight heard the note of pride in her mother's voice, and it warmed her just a little bit as she nodded.

"And a law degree too, I understand," Carrie said, and Midnight nodded again.

"So why don't you practice law instead of getting shot at?" Carrie asked, no degradation in her voice.

"I'm not into being a lawyer. I just wanted the law degree so I'd know who to bust and why. It comes in handy when I write warrants and the like."

"I see." Carrie pulled a chair over to Midnight's bed. She wanted to get to know her daughter. She was happy to have the chance to have an actual conversation with her. She reached over, touching Midnight's wedding ring.

"That is a beautiful ring," she said. Her own wedding ring was a mere chip. When she and Jack had rebelled against their parents and run off to get married, they certainly couldn't afford much, and they'd never thought to change the ring.

Midnight looked down at her hand, smiling as she remembered the night Rick had given it to her. "It was Rick's grandmother's. She had wanted him to give it to someone very special to him."

"Well, obviously you were that someone." Carrie saw a look cross Midnight's face. "What?"

"Yeah, I'm special alright," Midnight said, her voice dripping with sarcasm. "So special that after a little over three years of marriage he's cheating on me already."

Carrie stared openmouthed. "No way!"

"Way." Midnight nodded.

"Are you sure, or do you just think he's cheating on you?" Carrie's voice indicated that she still didn't believe it.

"Mother," Midnight said, for the first time without any sort of anger attached to it—Midnight didn't realize that, but Carrie noted it and clung to it hopefully. "The woman that called you, Angela Theland." Carrie nodded. "She's Rick's girlfriend's mother."

Carrie just stared at her daughter, totally confused now. "Why was she making the phone calls then?"

Midnight shrugged. "Maybe she was so happy about it, she wanted everyone to know. How do I know?"

"No," Carrie said, shaking her head. "She actually sounded upset about the idea of you dying."

"I doubt that."

"Well, I don't. It seems that your demise would be devastating for an awful lot of people around here."

Midnight didn't reply. She just looked at her mother for a long moment, then shook her head. She couldn't believe that it was her mother saying these things to her. She had to admit, it did feel good to have someone to talk to about this who wasn't directly involved.

****

Randy's trip to the apartment that she and Sarah shared took a lot longer than she had expected. She didn't know what she was going to say, or how she was going to act. She ended up driving around for two hours, trying to decide. It never occurred to her that Dick would be at the apartment, but when she drove up to the front, she saw his truck.

She sat in her car taking slow deep breaths for a few minutes, knowing that she was going to have to face Dick eventually. Now was as good a time as any. When she walked into the apartment, the first thing she saw was Dick sitting on the couch, watching TV. He looked up, and Randy tried to smile.

"Hi," she said weakly.

"Hi," he said, eyeing her. "Where've you been? Sarah said you haven't been home since Friday."

Randy shrugged, not wanting to answer him. She was taken aback when Dick stood up and walked over to her. She realized at that moment that she didn't know what she'd seen in him. He was so far away from what Joe was that she couldn't believe she had even been attracted to him. When he drew close to her, she found herself becoming afraid.

"Sarah tells me that you received a summons from Lieutenant Chevalier. That true?" His voice indicated that he knew it was.

Randy nodded.

"So what'd she say?"

Randy didn't answer; she moved around him and headed for the bedroom. She reached into the closet and pulled out her suitcase. She turned to see that Dick had followed her and was watching her expectantly from the doorway. His eyes followed the suitcase to the bed. "What did she say, Randy?" he repeated, this time a little more ominously.

"She said that she wasn't going to turn us in," Randy said simply as she began to pull her clothes out of dresser drawers.

"But you have to leave town by sundown?" Dick started to laugh. "Is that the deal you made with her? She'll let you keep your freedom if you leave?"

Randy just looked at him for a minute, finding it hard to believe that he was taking this so lightly. "After what you did, it's a wonder she isn't going to press charges," she said angrily. She turned back to the closet.

Dick strode over and grabbed her from behind, pinning her arms to her side. "What I did?" he said, his voice grating in her ears. "I don't think you're remembering it quite right. Don't you remember, you threw the first punch."

"I didn't do anything," Randy said shakily. "I missed her totally."

"Now see, that's not how I remember it, Your Honor. Randy Curtis-Sinclair even held Lieutenant Chevalier for me when I hit her. Randy Curtis-Sinclair wanted to get the lieutenant back for trying to ruin her career. She talked me into going over to the house—I didn't realize what she had in mind at the time. Things just got out of control, Your Honor, and I'm so sorry, but Randy Sinclair instigated the whole thing." Dick sounded innocent and honest, and Randy wanted to scream. Instead, she elbowed him roughly in the stomach. Dick doubled over, coughing, but recovered quickly. He grabbed Randy and threw her on the bed. Randy used her academy training, taking advantage of the momentum of Dick's strength to roll off the other side of the bed and get to her feet. Looking around quickly as Dick started to come around the bed, she grabbed the bat that Sarah kept in the room. She brandished it at Dick and eyed him threateningly.

"You won't use it," Dick said confidently.

"You wanna bet?" Randy replied. She sounded a lot like Midnight.

Dick nodded, his face a mask of superiority. "Oh yeah, I'll bet on it, because if you do hit me with it, I'll kill you." He sounded deadly serious, and that made Randy hesitate momentarily. She lowered the bat just slightly. Dick took advantage of the opportunity and lunged at her. Randy brought the bat up, striking him on the shoulder. Dick fell to the floor, and Randy ran out of the room, careful to avoid his arms as he reached out and tried to grab her legs. She dashed through the living room, dropping the bat as she ran out the door and down the stairs. She headed toward the front of the apartment complex, looking back to see if Dick was following her. She ran right into someone. She screamed, imagining that Dick had somehow managed to get ahead of her.

"Whoa!" Joe's voice surprised her. "Calm down!" Randy thought she'd die from relief. She threw her arms around him, clinging to him as if for dear life. Joe held her close, but he looked up at the apartment block just in time to see Dick coming out the front door. Dick stopped dead in his tracks when he saw Joe. Randy turned as Dick started down the stairs—she noticed that he was reaching behind him. She knew he was going for the weapon that he kept at the small of his back.

"Joe!" she yelled. "He's going for his gun!"

In one fluid motion, Joe shoved Randy behind him and drew his own weapon from his shoulder holster, just as Dick brought his gun up. They stood with their weapons pointed at each other.

"Drop it, Dickerson," Joe said sternly, "or I'll drop you."

"Go ahead and try it, Sinclair."

They stood staring at each other for a long time. Joe tilted his head to the side, as if making calculations. "I'd say we're about, oh, twenty to twenty-five yards apart. My best shot's about twenty-three yards. That gives you about a two-yard leeway," he said, his voice very calm and cool.

Randy stood watching the two men. She knew Dick would have no qualms about shooting a fellow officer, but she was sure that Joe would have a problem doing so unless given enough reason. Making a quick decision, she leaned down and started patting Joe's ankle, subsequently reaching up his pants leg and pulling out a particularly nasty-looking Walther PPK. She leveled it at Dick. "And if by chance he misses you, which I wouldn't count on, then I'm sure at least one of these seven shots'll hit you."

Joe's expression changed just slightly, as if saying to Dick, "See, even your girlfriend wants you shot." Dick stared at them both for a long few moments. Randy noticed Joe's finger tense on the trigger as he stared down the sights of his weapon. Finally Dick lowered his gun, and without a word he walked back up the stairs toward the apartment. Joe didn't lower his weapon until he saw Dickerson actually open the door, step inside, and close the door behind him.

Joe holstered his gun, then looked over at Randy. "You've been listening," he said proudly.

"Did I have a choice?" She smiled as she handed his backup to him.

"And you even remembered my favorite hiding place—that's love for ya."

"Oh yeah?" Randy said as they turned to walk toward their respective cars. "By the way, what made you show up here?" She had suddenly realized that it had been a pretty lucky chance.

"I called the house when I left the hospital, and when you weren't home, I got worried. I got Sarah's address from dispatch and headed over here." Joe shrugged, as if it were no big deal.

"Well, thanks."

Joe was looking at her closely. "You okay to drive?"

Randy nodded.

"I'll follow you." He kissed her quickly on the lips. Randy watched as he strode over to his car and got in. She was once again amazed at how he took everything in stride and just continued on. Her hands were still shaking from the confrontation. But she was very grateful to have her husband follow her back to their home. She thought she'd never want to leave it again.

The next morning, Randy was surprised that when she got up to get ready for the academy, Joe got up at the same time. They had spent a quiet evening the night before. Randy had been reluctant to discuss what had happened, since part of it had to do with Midnight being hurt. It bothered her immensely that she was hiding her part in Midnight's injury, but she knew that telling Joe now would only make things harder again. Joe hadn't asked what had happened, assuming that she would tell him if she wanted him to know. So they had ordered Chinese again, and had relaxed out on the deck with a bottle of wine. They'd gone to bed early, since Randy had to get up at 5:30 a.m. to be at the academy by 8:00 a.m. Joe hadn't mentioned getting up with her, but she didn't mind the company, nor the fact that he made her coffee for a change.

She was doubly surprised when she walked out into the kitchen after her shower and found that he had also showered, and was shaved and dressed. Joe was leaning against the kitchen counter, drinking his coffee and flicking through the paper. He glanced up at her when she walked in. She was wearing her academy uniform, and his eyes looked her over from head to toe. He gestured with his cup. "You might want to straighten that plum line," he said. Being a sergeant, he was used to inspection requirements, although he hadn't been subject to them for years.

Randy glanced down and saw that her belt was just slightly askew. She grinned up at him as she fixed it. "Guess having a sergeant for a husband could come in handy yet."

"Just what I was thinkin'." Joe tilted his head to the side. "Have you gotten your ride-along assignment yet?" he asked. He was surprised to see her tense, but he assumed it was because she thought he was going to be difficult about it.

After a few moments Randy shrugged, shaking her head. "I had applied for a ride-along assignment with FORS, but..." She trailed off, not wanting to really go into why it hadn't happened.

"I see," Joe said simply, nodding. "Midnight said no, huh?"

Randy looked at him, shocked, but then she realized that Midnight must have told him about her behavior at her lecture. She nodded, embarrassed.

"She was pretty pissed about that." Joe knew she knew what he was talking about.

"Tell me about it," Randy said. "I was sore for about a week." She rubbed her back to indicate where.

Joe laughed. "That'll teach you," he said, wagging his finger at her. "Anyway, I think as the acting commander for FORS I'll rescind that denial."

Randy stared at him, wondering if her mind was playing tricks on her. Her husband, the man who had been adamant about her not becoming a cop, wanted her to do a ride-along with his unit now? Then it dawned on her why.

"You figure I'll be safer with you than with some beat cop you don't know, right?" she said, but with no anger in her voice.

"You got it, babe," Joe said, without a hint of apology.

Randy just shook her head, grinning. "So where are you going this morning then?"

"First, I'm taking you to school and clearing this with your training sergeant, then I'm heading into the office to get things squared away." He looked at her again, this time with a mockingly shy expression. "Want to have lunch with an old training sergeant?"

Randy looked as if she was considering the idea carefully. "I don't know," she said finally. "I do have an image to uphold."

"What image is that?"

"The stupid broad that's dumb enough to let a gorgeous man like Sergeant Joe Sinclair go image," she replied simply, but her eyes indicated her mortification at her asinine actions.

Joe shook his head. "Randy, don't do that to yourself. You did what you felt was right at the time. I know I'm far from the perfect husband, and you put up with a lot of shit."

"Like what?" Randy said. She still doubted herself.

"Like all the late nights, or the nights I didn't come home at all because we worked on paperwork for so long I passed out on Midnight's couch. My relationship with my boss. My moods, my drinking sometimes." He looked at her pointedly. "Should I go on?"

"I knew I was marrying a cop, Joe. That's what you do, who you are. How can I find fault with that?"

Joe scratched the side of his face, studying her for a moment. "It's a lot easier to say than to do, Randy. I know that. Don't be so hard on yourself." He walked over to her and pulled her into an embrace, kissing the top of her head. "I love you, and I want you to be happy too. If being a cop will make you happy…" He shrugged, still holding her against him. "Then I'll just have to deal with that, 'cause I can't let you go."

Randy wanted to cry. Hearing him say it that way made her aware once again of how foolish she had been. She had realized a number of times over the last couple of days that she had come dangerously close to losing probably the most perfect man in the world. He loved her enough to give up some of himself to be with her, and that made him perfect. She also realized once again that she had Midnight to thank for making her snap out of her downward spiral. It just about made her sick to think about what Dick and she had done—she was sure the guilt would eat her alive. She told herself she would tell Joe soon, but inside she shrank from the idea of maybe losing him over something she really hadn't meant to happen. And if Midnight didn't want to tell Joe, her mind told her, why should she? She knew she was deluding herself again, but she refused to analyze the situation any closer.

A couple of hours later, Randy felt everyone's eyes on her as she got out of the black Porsche with the vanity plate that read "SNCLAIR." Everyone knew Joe's car; he had become kind of a legend as the cop who did the job because he loved it, even though he was rich and definitely didn't need the money. Joe got out of the car, shrugging into his FORS jacket, and escorted her to her class with his hand placed gently at the small of her back. Just outside the room, she turned to look up at him. She knew she couldn't kiss him, even if she really wanted to. He leaned down, his lips right next to her ear, but in a way that didn't appear too inappropriate—though Randy found that she was willing to get a black mark just to have him kiss her. He didn't.

"Be good," he whispered, allowing his lips to brush her ear softly. Randy shivered at the sensation it created. She was once again amazed by the effect he had on her. She couldn't believe that she'd ever grown used to him. Joe straightened as the academy sergeant came up.

"Hey, Sinclair," the man said, clapping Joe companionably on the back and eyeing Randy. This was a unique situation for Sergeant James Jones. Here was one of his cadets with her husband, who also happened to be a sergeant that he knew pretty well. It was further complicated by the fact that Jones knew about Randy's dalliance with another sergeant in the department, and he wasn't sure if Sinclair knew it too.

"How's the LT?" he asked Joe. He was curious about Midnight's condition but didn't want to act too casually in front of a cadet. Randy took the hint and went into the classroom, glancing back and smiling at Joe, whose eyes followed her until she was through the door. He looked back at the other sergeant.

"She's good," he said, nodding. "Look, I wanted to talk to you about Randy—I mean, Cadet Curtis." Joe made a face. He didn't like the use of her maiden name, but wasn't sure how to refer to her without making it sound too easygoing either. "Oh hell," he said, giving up. "I wanted to talk to you about my wife."

Sergeant Jones grinned at Joe, knowing it had to be difficult to balance a life with circumstances like his. Jones was aware, as much as many people in the department were, of Midnight and Joe's previous relationship as well as their continued closeness even though they were both married to other people, one of whom was a member of FORS. Jones imagined that things got more complicated indeed when divorce and infidelity came into play. "Okay, so talk." He gestured toward his office, a couple of doors away.

Joe followed him in, leaning casually against the door jamb as the other man sat down in his chair. "I wanted to ask about Randy's ride-along options."

Jones looked up at Joe, surprised that he wasn't aware of the situation with Randy's request to ride along with FORS. "Don't you and your boss talk at all?" he asked, shaking his head.

Joe nodded. "Well, yeah. I know that Midnight turned down Randy's request, but I'd like to rescind that denial."

Jones looked at him critically. "Midnight's a lieutenant, Joe. You can't countermand her order."

"I can if I'm acting in her stead right now," Joe replied calmly.

"Yes, technically you could," Jones said slowly. "But I don't think you realize how strongly she felt about this denial."

"Yeah, I think I do. But some things have changed since then, and I don't think it's an issue anymore." He looked at Jones. "Unless your office has a problem with it." He kept his voice amicable; he didn't want to step on any toes just yet.

Jones looked at Joe for a few moments, not sure if he was willing to fight this one. It was obvious that there were some underlying circumstances here, and in reality, if Joe was really acting in Midnight's place, he did have a right to countermand her order as long as he made her aware of it when she returned. It was not his place to decide how Midnight would "feel" about the countermand, just to make sure it was for all intents and purposes within regulations.

"No," he said finally. "I don't have a problem with it. I just didn't want you to get your ass in the fire."

Joe smiled. "Thanks, Jim. You know I don't do anything on a whim. If truth be known," he said confidentially, "I'd rather have my wife where I can keep an eye on her than out with some beat cop who already has too much to do to have to be overprotective of some sergeant's bride. Ya know?"

Jones nodded. "Yeah, I guess if I was still married I'd think that way too." He grinned. "Just glad I don't have your life, man."

"It does have its moments, I'll tell you that."

A half hour later, still in class, Randy received a message from Training Sergeant Jones that her ride-along with FORS had been approved. Grinning widely, she glanced over at Sarah and found her more or less glaring back. Randy knew there was going to be a problem there.

When they were released for lunch, Randy found that there was indeed a problem. Sarah strode up to her, glowering. "What the hell was this? I heard your husband pulled a gun on my brother?"

They were standing just outside the doorway to the classroom, and Randy glanced around, realizing to her relief that Joe wasn't there yet. She didn't want him involved in this too; he'd had to stick up for her too many times lately.

"Well, you've already got it wrong," Randy said calmly. "It was Dick that pulled the gun first—Joe was just matching his actions."

"Yeah? What was he doin' there in the first place?" It was a loaded question, and Randy knew Sarah really wanted to know if she and Joe were getting back together.

She blew her breath out in a sigh. "He was worried about me, and he came to find me. Dick and I had just finished a fight, and I was running out of the apartment as Joe walked up. Dick followed me, and when he saw Joe he pulled his weapon." It was a simplified version of the scene that had taken place, but it was the truth.

"That's not what he says," Sarah replied hotly.

"Yeah, well, I'll just bet that he doesn't always tell the truth when he's on the receiving end of humiliation."

"What's that supposed to mean?"

"It means that your brother acted like a coward," Randy said mildly.

Sarah looked at her sharply. She didn't like either her or her words—her brother was her hero, and she didn't stand for people putting him down. "He's a coward because he didn't shoot your estranged husband?" she said derisively.

"Hardly. He's a coward because he found it necessary to draw his weapon for no plausible reason."

"Your husband was reason enough. He's threatened to kill Dick, hasn't he?" Sarah sounded triumphant at having remembered that.

But Randy shrugged. "Sure, but that was when we were standing in his house and Dick was making nasty remarks about Midnight. In fact, Joe put his gun down that time, willing to take your brother on hand to hand, so I wouldn't say he was bent on killing him, no."

"You're all protective of him now, huh?"

"We're back together, if that's what you're asking." Randy saw Joe walking toward them. His eyes went to Sarah and then back to Randy, as if trying to decide whether to interrupt. His decision obviously made, he walked up to stand behind Randy and looked down at Sarah.

Sarah glared daggers up at him but said nothing. She looked back at Randy and shook her head. "I can see that much," she said, then turned on her heel and walked away.

Joe watched her go. "Nice girl," he muttered, and Randy glanced back at him.

"Dick told her that you drew down on him first yesterday," she said angrily.

Joe shrugged. "Figures," was all he had to say about the issue. "You ready?"

Randy nodded and followed him to the car. They went to lunch at a small Mexican restaurant close to the college. Joe didn't mention Dickerson, so Randy didn't either. She was still fuming, however, about Dick's twisting of the truth. She could see him so clearly now, and it made her sick to think that she had almost given up Joe for him. It would have been like giving up Prince Charming for the frog.

Joe dropped Randy back at the academy, telling her he'd be there on time to pick her up. Randy nodded. "You probably haven't been on time a day in your life," she said, grinning. "But I'll wait for you."

Joe laughed and flipped her a wave as he drove off. He dropped by the hospital on the way back to the office. Midnight looked better again, and the doctors were saying that if she kept up the progress, they'd maybe let her go home the following week. Midnight made a face when they told her she would have to rest at home if she was released. Dr. Duhane, who had grown fond of his spirited patient, had warned her that he'd even go so far as to make a surprise house-call-slash-inspection to make sure she was taking it easy, and if she wasn't he'd bounce her right back to the hospital.

"I'll be there to keep an eye on her and make sure she doesn't overdo it," Carrie said, surprising Joe and Midnight. But what surprised Joe more was the fact that Midnight did not protest vehemently. Obviously he'd missed something. He made a mental note to catch up with her soon. He headed back to FORS.

The office was chaotic, as usual, and Joe waded through the memos and paperwork on Midnight's desk. By five thirty, he was basically running to get out of there. He shocked Randy by pulling up to the curb in front of the college at exactly 6:00 p.m. On the way home, they talked easily about what she had learned at the academy, and Joe got a chance to unload all of the problems he was having at the office.

"What I need is a secretary," he said, raising an eyebrow at her. "I had one, but she ran away."

Randy clicked her tongue, shaking her head. "Boy can't count on anyone these days, can you?"

"Tell me about it," Joe said, grinning now.

At Randy's direction, Joe stopped at the local grocery store and they picked up food. Randy had admonished him, because she knew he'd be happy to live off takeout food, but if she continued to eat Chinese and the like she'd never make it over the six-foot wall for the physical agility part of the academy.

"I'm having a hard enough time with that damn wall as it is," she said, grimacing.

"You just have to know the trick, that's all," Joe said.

"There's a trick?"

"Yes, love, there's a trick to everything." Joe sounded like the wise old owl.

"Well, where the hell have you been?"

"Sacramento."

Randy looked at him, trying to decide if there was any leftover anger in his voice, but she couldn't tell. Joe was pretty good at hiding his emotions when he wanted to.

After a few long minutes Randy turned to him, stopping in the middle of the aisle. "I know that it will probably cause some of your circuits to short out," she said, her voice hopeful, "but would it be too much to ask if I wanted your help getting through some of this?" Her teeth worried her lower lip as she watched for his reaction.

Joe looked at her sharply at first, as if surprised that she'd even ask, but then he started to nod slowly. "Yeah, I think I could." He didn't sound particularly enthusiastic, but Randy hadn't even expected him to say yes.

She reached up and kissed him on the lips, and what was meant to be a quick thank you turned into something a little bit more. Joe pulled her close to him and returned her kiss with a long, playful one of his own. Randy let out a giggle as he picked her up off her feet, and she immediately wrapped her legs around his waist as they continued to kiss. Everyone in the aisle watched, some enviously, others with amusement. One older couple thought it was the sweetest thing they'd seen in a long time. When the kiss ended, Joe looked down at Randy with a wide grin. She smiled back up at him. It was good to be together again, and they both reveled in the feeling.

****

That evening, Rick was having dinner with his parents. They had gotten into the habit over the last few days, and in two more days the senior Debenshires were returning home. The conversation had started out light. They'd talked about Midnight's progress, and Rick told them what the doctor had said about releasing her the following week.

"You definitely married a fighter there," Robert said, amazed that in three short days Midnight had gone from almost dead to recovering nicely.

Rick nodded seriously. "Tell me about it."

Robert looked at his son for a long moment. "She doesn't want to take you back, does she?" His voice was firm but sympathetic.

Rick shook his head miserably.

"Have you talked to her?" Anabelle asked.

"I don't need to," Rick said. "Midnight has a way of making her feelings known. She doesn't want me around." He sounded devastated, and Anabelle reached out to pat his hand softly.

"Maybe she just needs some time. This hasn't exactly been a good few weeks for her."

"I know, Mum," Rick said, his face still somber. "But hard times were always the times we turned to each other. But now…" He trailed off as he shook his head again.

"So what are you going to do about it?" Robert asked.

Rick looked at his father blankly. "What can I do?" He sounded like the young boy he had been years before, when he'd broken a toy and needed his father's help fixing it.

"Richard," Robert said, his eyes softening, though his voice remained firm. "You love her, don't you?"

"Yes," Rick said, shaking his head miserably. "I actually wish I could say no and be honest, but she's like breathing—without her, I'm dead."

"You need to tell her that," Robert said.

"It's not that easy, Dad. You have no idea how good Midnight can be about ignoring every word you say. She's like a light switch—she can shut her feelings off totally."

"I don't believe that," Anabelle said. "I think she's good at making you think that, but she loves you, Richard. Midnight Chevalier didn't strike me as the type to marry someone on a whim."

"She's not. She did love me." Rick scrubbed at his face, frustrated. "But I screwed that up."

"Yes, you did," Robert said. "And now you have to deal with the consequences. But if your wife is worth anything, you need to fight for her."

"She doesn't want me anymore."

"How do you know?" Anabelle said.

"Because I know who she wants." Rick sounded defeated.

"And who would that be?" Robert asked. "Joe?"

Rick looked shocked by his father's words. "How do you know that?"

"Richard," Anabelle said, touching his hand gently, "your father and I know all about Joe and Midnight's relationship. What the two of you didn't tell us your sisters filled in. But I think you're very wrong."

"And how do you know?" Rick snapped, feeling angry and raw.

Anabelle stared at her son, not used to his short temper. "Richard," she said, her tone cautionary.

"I'm sorry. Look, I really need to get some air. I'll be back." Rick stood and strode to the front door of the restaurant. Outside, he stood leaning against the wall. He didn't want to go back. He didn't want to talk about Midnight—he didn't want to think about not being with her anymore. He wanted to be alone with his thoughts.

Rick walked back into the restaurant and up to the front desk, where he asked for a piece of paper. He pulled out his pen and scribbled a note to his parents, telling them that he didn't feel well and he was going home.

That night, he sat in the house that he and Midnight had shared for three and a half years and got quietly drunk. He ended up passing out on the couch. He woke the next morning feeling awful. He went to the bathroom and found some aspirin in the medicine cabinet. As he turned the lid, he noticed blood on the bottle. He looked at it for a long time, and started to think about everything that had happened in the last two months or so. He thought about the fights and the anger, and then he thought about what had happened before that. He realized that he had allowed himself to become so angry over Midnight's success that it had eaten at him to the point that he wanted something just for himself. Then along came Sheila Theland. Sheila still wanted him from so many years ago; she hung on his every word. In her world he was the rich playboy. He was important. The attraction to Sheila had been what she could give him—attention, notoriety, almost fame, in a way. He could be part of something again, and not just some guy who was lucky enough to be married to Lieutenant Chevalier. He also realized that he still wanted that in some way. He wanted to get away from all of the things that were going wrong with his life, and Sheila had been a logical means to that end. Then he'd managed to convince himself that Midnight was sleeping with Griff. He remembered the night Joe had found him at Sheila's; he had tried to blame Midnight for being there, but even then he knew he was wrong. But it just didn't seem to matter. And now here he was, losing the one woman he really loved. Without thinking about it any further, Rick walked into the bedroom and picked up the phone. He dialed Sheila's number.

When Sheila came on the line he told her they needed to talk and to come over to the house. Sheila agreed and was there twenty minutes later.

When Rick opened the front door, Sheila knew she wasn't going to like the discussion they were about to have, but she was also sure she could change his mind.

"Sheila, sit down," Rick said, but she shook her head and went to kiss him. Rick stood like a stone statue, looking down at her, his eyes cold. Sheila tried smiling up at him, but it had no effect. Finally, she went to the couch and sat down. He walked over to the bar and took a quick shot of brandy. He turned to her, but he saw something in her eyes, and before he could say another word, before she even opened her mouth, he knew what she was going to say. She had a glint in her eyes that told him she had plans for him, no matter what he thought.

Rick narrowed his eyes at her. "What is it?" he asked, knowing the answer.

"Well, I'm not totally sure," she said sweetly, "but I think I might be pregnant."

Rick's face changed instantly, from quizzical to stone. "Well, that's unfortunate for you. Because I don't care."

"What do you mean, you don't care?" she said, her eyes shining with tears.

"I think you know what I mean," Rick said coldly. "But let me lay it out for you. I'm married, Sheila, and since I am, I can't and won't marry you."

"But your wife has filed for a divorce," Sheila supplied helpfully.

Rick's eyes narrowed. "Filed, yes. Got, no."

"Well, Richard, you don't think she's just going to sit around and wait for you to sign some silly papers, do you? In this country, you don't have to sign anything. If she doesn't want anything from the marriage, she can walk away."

"She can't walk away with Mikeyla."

"No, but if she decides to give you custody, she can be gone."

"She wouldn't do that," Rick said, though he sounded less sure.

Sheila shrugged. "Maybe not, but I wouldn't count on it."

Rick stared at her, wondering how he had managed to get snared in her web again.

The next morning, Rick walked into Joe's office, kicking the door closed with a booted foot and sitting down heavily in the chair in front of Joe's desk.

"Good morning to you too," Joe said wryly.

"Yeah, right," Rick replied sullenly.

"Problems?" Joe's voice indicated he had an idea what one of those might be.

Rick eyed his best friend, wondering what Joe knew. "Some. What do you know?"

"I know you and Midnight are still on the outs," Joe said bluntly.

"That's a safe way to put it. She hates me, is a better way of putting it."

Joe shook his head. "I thought we already covered this ground."

"Well, whatever reason she had for wanting to keep my baby seems to have died with it," Rick said candidly. "She won't talk to me—she won't tell me anything. Whenever I'm around she clams up and makes a point of sleeping a lot. And now…" He trailed off, not sure how Joe was going to take the latest twist in his life.

"What?" Joe asked suspiciously.

Rick shook his head. He closed his eyes for a minute, as if he couldn't believe this new information himself. Opening his eyes again, he looked straight into Joe's. "Sheila thinks she's pregnant."

Joe stared at him for a long moment, and to Rick's shock, started to laugh and shake his head ruefully. "Christ, man, you don't fucking learn, do you?" He sounded disbelieving. "Here you are, it's been years, and yet Sheila's got you by the balls again." He looked at him disdainfully. "Didn't you pay attention last time?"

"Don't start with me, Joe," Rick said, irritated more with himself than his friend. "Don't you think I've thought the same thing over and over?"

"So?"

"So what? You don't think I'm daft enough to marry her, do you? Even if I could."

"Oh, you could."

"What's that supposed to mean?"

"Just that Midnight isn't the kind of person to sit around pining for you for the rest of her natural life." He looked at Rick seriously. "That baby may have been your last chance to get her back."

"God, man, don't say that," Rick said, hanging his head miserably.

"You want me to lie?" Joe knew the answer even before Rick shook his head. "Alright then. So now what are you going to do? You gonna tell Midnight?"

"Do you think I should?"

"I wouldn't."

"But what if she finds out some other way? She'll kill me then."

"That's true enough. Maybe you should tell her there's a chance. I mean, hell, she's not even sure, right?"

"Yeah," Rick said. "Just like last time."

"Think she's lying?"

Rick shrugged. "Could be. I still think she was lying the first time, or at least exaggerating a day-late period."

"Well, it's up to you whether or not to tell Midnight. But I wouldn't want to be in your shoes if you don't tell her and someone like Angela slips."

"Honesty's the best policy—is that what you're telling me?"

Joe nodded.

"A minute ago you said you wouldn't tell her. Now you've changed your mind?"

"I've been known to do that," Joe said, shrugging. "Look, thinkin' about it, I can see that there's been too much shit you two haven't told each other, and I just think it's time you started bein' straight with one another, okay?"

Rick gave him a sour look. "I hate it when you're so goddamned logical."

Joe grinned. "Cool, ain't it?"

Later that day, Rick went over to the hospital. His heart was in his throat as he walked to Midnight's room. He knocked lightly and pushed open the door. He was surprised that Carrie wasn't there. It had taken a little getting used to, that Midnight and her mother seemed to be getting along better now.

Midnight glanced up at him; she had been reading some papers, and she set them aside. Rick could see something different in her eyes, and he wondered what the papers were. He knew Joe had put a moratorium on anyone smuggling work into her, and he was sure no one would be brave enough to defy Joe at this point. As his eyes went to the pages now lying on the bed stand, Midnight pointedly picked them up and turned them over so he couldn't read anything. He looked at her, trying to work out what she was trying to hide from him now.

"We have to talk," Rick said, sitting down on the edge of the bed. Again, Midnight made a point of moving away from him. She looked at him blankly, and then nodded her head, as if telling him he could continue. Rick hesitated, not wanting to tell her what he'd come to say when she was very obviously not in the mood to hear anything at all. He knew, though, that there wasn't going to be a right time to tell her about Sheila, and the longer he waited, the more likely it was she'd find out from someone else.

"What is it we have to talk about?" Midnight asked finally when he didn't say anything.

"Us," Rick said simply, and then shrugged. "And other things."

His voice was overly casual, and Midnight picked up on it immediately. "What other things?"

Rick drew in a deep breath, wishing he could be anywhere but here right now. He looked into her eyes, somewhat glad that she didn't have her firearm handy. "Sheila thinks she might be pregnant," he said, his voice the only sound in the room.

Rick saw a pained look cross Midnight's face, but then her mask of cool disdain dropped over her again. "That's ironic," she said.

"What's ironic?" Rick said, angry at her frosty response. "That she might be pregnant, or that I might be the father?"

"Neither, actually." Midnight's voice was still even. She shrugged. "Maybe it's for the best," she said with forced lightness. "Maybe you'll get a son this time, someone to carry on the Debenshire name."

"Midnight!" Rick yelled, his anger burning hot now. He was unable to comprehend how she could be so cold and unfeeling about such an inflammatory issue. He stood and started pacing, throwing her angry looks as he tried to walk off the outrage coursing through his veins. Could she really despise him so much, to take something like the woman he was seeing being pregnant so calmly? "Do you really hate me now? Is that it?"

"What's that got to do with Sheila being pregnant?" Midnight asked levelly, watching him as he paced.

Rick stopped, staring at her in disbelief. He could not accept that she was saying all this. "It has nothing to do with Sheila and everything to do with us," he said, exasperated to have to spell this out to her.

"Oh, I'd say that if Sheila's pregnant, it has a lot to do with us."

"Why?" Rick asked blankly.

Midnight gave a hollow laugh. "Apparently you've really given this a lot of thought."

"Oh, I've thought about it—you can count on it."

"And you haven't come to the conclusion that it affects us?"

"Jesus Christ, Midnight, I'm not an idiot. I know it affects us, but you hating me shouldn't have anything to do with it."

Midnight made a face, making it clear she thought he was crazy. "Just how did she maybe get pregnant, Rick? Through osmosis? I don't think so. You screwed her, and now she might be pregnant. If you think I'm going to congratulate you and note the kid's due date on my calendar, it's not gonna happen."

Rick narrowed his eyes at her, not enjoying being on the receiving end of her sharp tongue. "That's not what I meant, and you damn well know it. What I asked was if you hate me now."

"I think hate would be a fair assessment of my feelings for you and Sheila right now."

"I see." Rick felt like his heart had just been cut out. Midnight didn't reply; she just looked at him as if waiting for the other shoe to drop. "I won't marry her, if that's what you're wondering."

Midnight's expression didn't change. "Bully for you," she said, without any emotion whatsoever.

"You can be a real bitch sometimes, you know that?" Rick retorted, his eyes flashing angrily.

"So I've heard." Midnight sighed. "But I think it's warranted this time."

"Yeah, I'll just bet you do." The look on Rick's face changed to one of malicious anger. "You goin' back to Joe now or what?" The thought had just occurred to him, and fury flooded his veins.

But Midnight shook her head. "He and Randy are back together," she said simply, refusing to be drawn into another argument about Joe.

"So what're you going to do?" he said, confused now.

Midnight laughed sarcastically. "Believe it or not, I did just fine before I met either of you."

"Griffin?" Rick asked, anger still prevalent in his voice.

"Rick," Midnight said vindictively, "if you're looking for someone to blame, look in a mirror."

Rick had no reply to that one. He knew she was right. He walked out of the room, closing the door quietly behind him. Midnight stared up at the ceiling with tears in her eyes as she fought the urge to run after him. Her anger and her pride held her there, making her burn with the desire to find Sheila Theland and kill her slowly and painfully. Rick's infidelity was bad enough, but Randy's betrayal of Joe and of Midnight herself was unbelievable. Midnight didn't know how this was all going to turn out, but she knew she'd take care of her own, no matter what treachery was rising.

ACKNOWLEDGEMENTS

Thank you to Bill Yourczek for his very precise assistance where weapons are concerned. Thanks for all the help!!!

You can find more information about the author and series here:

www.sherrylhancock.com

www.facebook.com/SherrylDHancock

www.vulpine-press.com/midknight-blue-series

Also by Sherryl D. Hancock:

The *WeHo* series follows a group of women from Los Angeles as they navigate the ups and downs of love, life, work, and everything in between.

www.vulpine-press.com/we-ho

The *Wild Irish Silence* series. Escape into the world of BJ Sparks and discover how he went from the small-town boy to the world-famous rock star.

www.vulpine-press.com/wild-irish-silence-series